I'd like to thank my agent, Faith H. Childs, and my editor, Stacy Creamer, for their advice and expertise. I'd also like to thank Rosemarie Robotham, Joy Cain, Regina Joseph, Benilde Little, Lieutenant Hugh Holton, Chicago PD, and Jomo Ray for their additional help and support. And of course, as always, my husband, Richard.

Oh, the sinner man he gambled,
he gambled and fell:
He wanted to go to heaven,
but he had to go to hell.
There's no hiding place down here.

TRADITIONAL

For my daughter, Thembi, who always gives me strength

One

A fish sandwich was the only thing I had on my mind that night. A fried whiting sandwich, to be exact, from a smoky, fish-fry joint just off Central Avenue in Newark. I could almost taste its crisp, greasy goodness slapped between two slices of soft white bread with a mess of greens on the side, a tiny cup of Red Devil hot sauce tossed in the bag for the hell of it, and a pale dab of tartar sauce smeared on the far edge of the plate just to tempt me.

That fish sandwich damn near got me killed.

I didn't hear him coming, tipping on the toes of his shoes, like somebody's ghost. I didn't hear the sharp breath he must have taken or see the way his eyes shifted from one side of the parking lot to the other to make sure we were alone. I didn't smell trouble coming. But I felt it – the nose of his gun ramming into the middle of my spine, the way it shook when his hand did.

'Give it up, bitch!' It was a kid's voice. High and whispery, not even deepened into manhood or cracking yet like my son Jamal's did. It took me a minute to get it together – that soft voice and the hard metal thing wedged up against my back.

'I told you to give it up! Did you hear me?'

He said 'Did you hear me?' like his mama probably said it to him, wavering between threat and violence – a kid being

1

mannish, showing off. I stiffened, as scared as he probably was. Maybe more.

The street was empty, the parking lot dim. It was close to midnight. I'd been working late, making some last-minute notes on a surveillance case so I could give my final report to the client along with my bill. I'd walked into the parking lot hungry and drag-ass tired, not even aware of how dark it was. On its good days, the cheap lot near my PI's office has maybe two dull spotlights, but there was only one shining tonight, throwing its gleam about two feet on either side. I'd been walking toward my car, fumbling for my keys in the bottom of my bag, when he stopped me. I stood stiff now, sweat sliding down my back, clutching the leather strap of my bag so tight it hurt my hand.

'What do you want? My money? Keys? Here.' I thrust my red and green Kenya bag behind me, not waiting for an answer, hoping it would knock him off balance. It knocked against him, and his gun went deeper into my back as he snatched my bag and emptied it on the ground between us. My things hit the ground and something broke.

Damn it! My thirty-dollar Guerlain blusher! I thought, and in the same moment realised that nothing mattered but this boy with his gun poked into my spine. I pulled away from him. He stayed with me.

'Get it!'

'Get what?'

'The shit out your bag, the shit out your bag! Get it!'

Get it yourself, you little bastard.

'Okay.' My voice broke like a scared girl's does. I hated to show my fear to him. I steadied it. 'I've got to turn around to pick it up. Okay?' I said it like I'd say it to my own son, like I was explaining something to him he might not understand. My heart was beating fast, my mouth dry. But I knew he was scared

2

too. I knew it because his voice shook, and I know how a frightened boy sounds. The gun was shaking now too as he rocked it back and forth in the middle of my back. A scared kid is the last person in the world you want holding a gun on you. None of it's real to him: not you, not the gun, nothing. He'll pop you quicker than he'll pop a stick of gum.

'I'm going to step forward now. Okay?'

Silence.

'I want to get the things out of my bag so that I can give them to you.'

He took a breath as if he was unsure.

'Okay.' His voice was irritable but easy. I felt a rush of relief.

I turned around and stooped down, catching a quick look at him in the dim streetlight, putting a face and body with the kid voice.

He was taller than that voice had sounded but still shorter than me by about five inches, and I outweighed him by a good thirty pounds. Thin, slightly stooped shoulders and a skinny neck made him look like a young bird of prey. His skin was that dull, flat brown that comes from a diet of chocolate drink and orange soda instead of milk and orange juice. He was dressed the way kids dress on gangsta videos – how my son might dress if he could get out the house without my catching him – with a swagger and a fuck-you attitude: baggy jeans drooping low off his butt, black bubble jacket, unlaced Timberlands, head shaved clean to the scalp. A boy looking like inmates look in the joint, like he knew he had nothing waiting for him but prison or the graveyard. Jailhouse chic.

I stood back up to face him now, my wallet and keys in my hand. He had a boy's face, what I could see of it, not even the hint of a mustache on his upper lip. I wondered if he caught hell in the schoolyard or on the corner for a soft little face like that.

'If you take these from me now, it's a felony. You can do some serious time, if you take this out my hand.' Looking this boy in the face, I wasn't afraid of him. How old was he? Twelve? Thirteen? I wondered if the gun was real. I'd heard about that, kids like this breaking bad with a gun that isn't really a gun. It was big enough to be real – it looked like a Colt, snub-nosed and definitely a .38, but I'd seem toys that looked like that. They look real these days, get them started early.

'Do you understand me? It's a felony.'

He looked lost for a moment, as if he didn't quite get it, his face still obscured in shadow.

'If they hear about it.'

My hair stood up on the back of my neck. My stomach dropped.

'So you don't think they'll hear about it?' I found my voice and forced it out strong. Damned if I was going to let a skinny kid take away my voice. But even as I spoke, I thought about something I'd read a while back in the *Star-Ledger* about a woman who had tried to touch the conscience of a kid who she feared was going to kill her. She had tried to reason with him as he drove around with her in the passenger seat of her new car, talking to him, pleading with him, reasoning with him, and damned if he didn't kill her anyway, despite everything she'd said. Just for the hell of it. Just because he felt like it. She'd ended up as dead as if she'd cussed him out. As dead as I could end up. I studied his baby face and the gun that he had lowered now so it pointed at my heart. But I sensed something about this kid, a hesitancy and uncertainty. I decided to take a chance.

'First time you've done something like this?'

He looked at me like I'd lost my mind.

'Here.' I tossed the keys at him, surprising him; he jumped back as if they were hot or I'd taken a punch at him, and they hit the ground with a metal tinkle. 'You want my car? Take it.'

He paused the way a kid does, unsure of himself, studying the keys that lay on the ground between us like he'd never seen a set of keys before, not sure what his next move should be. I realised then that he wasn't going to use the gun. If he was, he would have done it when I threw the keys at him suddenly as I had. That disrespect would have cost me my life if he was ready to kill me, if any little excuse would do.

He was alone, which was a good thing. There was no crew to back him up, to show off for. No one to be embarrassed in front of. No chance for macho bonding or bragging, and that was what it would be about in the end. I wouldn't have had a chance if one of the boys had been riding backup with him, had seen me dis him like that, throwing those keys at him like I'd just done. It was just me and him, here together in the parking lot. If he wanted my car and money he had them now. He'd gotten what he came for. He could tell any tale he wanted to tell to anybody he wanted to tell it to now, and there was nobody to set things straight, to say how things had really gone down.

He glanced down at the keys, his eyes not leaving mine, the gun still on me. Then he knelt down and felt around the ground, forgetting the wallet I still held in my hand. He stood back up, clutching the keys.

'What one is yours?' His voice was shaking. I could hear his excitement. He wanted this to be over as much as I did.

I pointed to my car, which my son, Jamal, sarcastically calls the 'Blue Demon'. It's a faded blue diesel Jetta, which saw its best days ten years ago. Rust spots have settled on its hood like chickenpox, and there is a crack shaped like an egg in the passenger side's window. Twisted wire hangers have replaced vital parts: one is twisted into a figure of eight and sprouts from the hole in the hood that used to hold the antenna, but I can get any FM station in a radius of fifty miles. Its twin, which has kept me from the Midas muffler man for the last six weeks, props up the exhaust pipe so it won't drag on the ground. The kid took one look at my car, and his mouth dropped open.

'That!' He said the word like Jamal says it, squealing in a long, disgusted cry of outrage. I answered him the way I answer my son, with that blend of sad resignation and acceptance that only no bucks and life kicking your ass can bring.

'That.'

'You telling me that fucked-up piece of junk is your ride?'

'That's what I'm telling you.'

'Oh, shit!'

'What did you think I was driving, that Benz over there?' I risked a sarcastic comment and nodded towards a sleek silver Mercedes that clung to the curb and belonged to a small-time local hustler who did business in a club down the street. He looked at me and then at my Jetta and then back at me in dismay, realising in that terrible second that he had broken the first and only rule that thieves have: know what you're stealing.

He was obviously an amateur. He'd probably gotten into this mess spur of the moment, mad at somebody – his mama, his junior-high girlfriend. He'd taken me on with this gun he got from somewhere and climbed in deeper than he'd meant to.

But he was in it now.

I stepped slightly away from him, glancing around to see if

help was anywhere to be seen, praying that Mr Hustler would round the bend. The kid moved toward me suddenly, and I felt a thin line of sweat like a wet string drip from the nape of my neck down my spine.

He would need to save face.

'Give it to me.'

'You got it.'

'You know what I mean. The money. Give me the money. Bitch!' He spat that one word out, making it sound as mean and as ugly as I'd ever heard it sound, and that scared the hell out of me because I could hear the contempt and shame in his voice. Contempt for me because I was at his mercy and shame that he didn't know what he should have known, and that combination will make you kill as quick as fear. He was getting ready to make his second-chance move, his I don't-want-to-feel-a-chump play.

'Give it to me!'

The gun was back at my heart, the look of menace back on his baby face.

'You want my money?' I stalled.

'What the fuck else do you think I want.'

I had exactly six dollars and fifty cents in my wallet. I knew it because I'd counted it out before I left the office. Just enough for that fish sandwich I'd been dreaming about. I knew he would kill me because there wasn't more. Because he would have blown it twice on what was probably his first time out on a woman who was old enough to be his mama. Older than his mama probably, and in the end, saving face was all it was going to be about. He had a gun, and now he was going to have to shoot somebody with it, just to prove he wasn't a punk, to prove it to himself. I knew that simple truth as clearly as I knew my name.

So I said the three words that I knew might buy me some time.

'I'm a cop.' They rolled out of my mouth with every bit of threat I could put in them, like I was telling the truth, even though I haven't been a cop for almost a decade. I don't even like most cops much. But if he wasn't sharp enough to check out a car before he stole the keys, he wasn't sharp enough to ask for the badge I didn't have in my wallet. Nobody was stupid enough to shoot a cop. I could tell by the look that had settled on his face that he knew it.

'We're staking this lot out. My partner will be here before you get that gun back in your drawers good.' I lied fast and sure, my voice matter-of-fact. 'Why do you think I'm up in your punk-ass little face like this? That I'm not scared of you? How long you think it's going to take them to find you? You're getting ready to throw your life away over a couple of bucks and a car older than your mama. Nobody *ever* gets away with shooting a cop.'

He swallowed hard. I could see his Adam's apple bob in his throat.

'Put the gun away, son.'

Son.

He looked up at me. I could see his face fully in the dim light. He had high cheekbones, strong and prominent and full, pretty sweetheart lips. His eyes were hazel – brownish golden eyes in dark brown skin. It was a boy's face that might grow into that of a good-looking man, a heartbreaking kind of man. And in that moment I knew it was a face from my past, a blur from somewhere distant and painful.

I know this boy.

'Did you hear me, son?'

Where do I know this boy from?

8

He stared at me hard, his eyes wide with something I couldn't read. Then he turned tail and ran, his sneakers pounding the asphalt like he was being chased by the devil.

Two

I saw those same high cheekbones and light eyes later that week. I'd just finished my lunch, a disgusting excuse for a tuna fish sandwich I'd thrown together with too much fat-free mayonnaise and washed down with a cup of instant tomato soup. I'd decided to treat myself to a chocolate doughnut and coffee from the Dunkin' Donuts across the street, when I heard the knock on the door.

The woman looked to be in her early sixties; it's hard to tell with sisters. Her hazel eyes were rimmed with smudged eyeliner scrawled across the bottom of her lower lid like she didn't give a damn. Her fingernails were bitten off and sparsely covered with bright red polish, and she kept touching her lips with the tips of her skinny fingers as if she wasn't sure she wanted to let her words out. She perched on the edge of the chair across from me like she might want to get out in a hurry. I couldn't place her face any more than I'd been able to place the kid's, but I recognised those same high cheekbones and those light eyes.

She was dressed in a lime-green maid's uniform that was too big for her, and her short black hair looked like she'd whacked it off in disgust. She spoke fast, nervously, her words spilling out from between her thin, fluttering fingers.

'You don't remember me, do you? I know you from long

11

time ago. Way long time ago. You was a kid then, Tamara Hayle, just breaking into womanhood. You don't remember me, but that's okay. The years done changed me good.'

She took a pack of Newports out of her pocket, ripped off the wrapper, shook the cigarette out, looked around the room for a can to throw the paper in, and then finally stuffed it back into the black box of a pocketbook she'd placed on my desk. She lit the cigarette quickly, took a long, fast drag as if she'd been waiting for it all day, and then glanced at me, an apology in her eyes.

'You mind?'

I hate cigarettes, but she looked like she needed one and I was on her dime, so I didn't object.

'Bessie. Bessie Raymond,' she said through the smoke, in a voice that sounded like it had touched too many of what she'd just stuck in her mouth. 'Don't ring a bell, do it?'

I smiled politely. 'Sorry, it doesn't. What can I do for you, Ms Raymond?'

'You got a nice place here, Tamara Hayle. Real nice.' She glanced around my office, admiration in her eyes, which told me more about her than she probably wanted me to know.

'Nice' is not the word most folks use to describe my office. Functional, if you're kind. Tacky, if you're truthful. Tamara Hayle Investigative Services, Inc., the PI firm I founded a while back, is located on the second floor of a broken-down wreck of a building owned by my friend Annie. The walls of my office, basically a large square room with carpeting that Annie picked up cheap at a fire sale, are painted a dull grayish brown or brownish gray, depending on your mood when you walk in. Two windows, which haven't opened since the Italians ran city hall, are covered with a dreary film of unknown origin, and what I call my 'orphan aloe', an aloe plant that I inherited from an unknown donor, sits on the edge of the right windowsill. My desk, which I got at a yard sale about five years ago, is surrounded by three chairs, only two of which match. Everything in my place – from my file cabinet, which only opens when you kick it right, to the ancient table in the corner, to my computer, which takes a good twenty minutes to warm up before it boots up – belonged to somebody else.

My office is mine and I love it, but it is definitely not 'nice', and for one tense moment, I thought Bessie Raymond was trying to get smart with me, but her eyes told me she was on the level; they didn't have it in them to mock somebody just for the hell of it. They looked tired, like she hadn't gotten enough sleep or had spent the night crying.

'Would you like some tea, Ms Raymond?' She seemed uptight. I figured some herbal tea might cool her out; it always does me. I keep an electric kettle filled with water, some cups, a box of sugar cubes, instant coffee (for guests – I hate the mess!), and some Celestial Seasonings herbal teas on the small table. On second thought, she didn't really seem like the Celestial Seasonings type. 'Some coffee maybe?' I added. She shook her head no and dropped her eyes to her lap. 'Is there something you wanted to talk to me about? Something I can do for you?'

She glanced at her watch, and I reflexively looked down at mine. It was going on two. If she was on her lunch break she didn't have much time left – unless she worked the night shift, and was on her way home. Those tired eyes said that was a good possibility.

'I want you to find out who killed my boy.'

I paused, then said, 'That's a job for the police, Ms Raymond. That's not the kind of work I do.'

'The police?' She snorted contemptuously. 'Now you know

13

as well as me that the goddamn cops don't give a shit about people like me. About people like my son.' There was a bitterness in her voice that told me she knew what she was talking about.

'And you've come to me because you think I can do more than the police? I'm sorry, Ms Raymond, but I don't know how much I can help you.' I'm a private investigator, not a cop. I have my strengths, but solving crimes that the cops are supposed to isn't one of them. I can follow folks anywhere they want to take me, get information faster than the proverbial MF, but I know my limitations.

'I got money to pay.' She took out a thick bank envelope that said I was her first stop after the bank teller, and glared at me with the determination that only die-hard conviction brings. 'You can help me. You got to help me. I ain't leaving here until you say you will.'

'Why don't you tell me some more.' The least I could do was hear what the woman had to say.

'Somebody out there killed my son and I want to find out who did it.' There was nothing in her eyes when she said it, not anger, pain, or despair.

'I'm sorry, Ms Raymond.'

'What you got to be sorry for? You didn't have nothing to do with it.'

'And you said you went to the police?'

'That's what I said.'

'And now you're coming to me . . .' I let her finish the question.

'Because I owe it to my boy and I owe it to my son's babies.'

'Your grandchildren.'

'Yeah.'

'How long ago was he killed?'

'He been dead going on seven months now. He was killed on April twenty-fifth. Seven months ago today. It's taken me damn near seven months to even be able to talk about it good. The cops said they tried to find out who did it, but you know that don't mean shit. My boy opened his door one Thursday night and let in somebody who shot him dead. Just like somebody shot his daddy. It was around midnight, they said, just like that song his daddy used to like. "Round Midnight", just like that. They found him a couple of hours later.'

'Who found him?'

'The super in his building.'

'And he was the one who called the police?'

'Yeah.'

'And then they called you?'

'Then they called me.'

'So you went right over when they called?'

'Yeah.'

'And what exactly did the police say?'

'Niggers killing niggers.'

'They said that?' I asked, the old rage about the way cops treat people who look like me, who look like Bessie Raymond, boiling up in me again.

'They didn't have to say it. That was what was in their eyes.'

'Had your son been in trouble with the law?' *Had be been in trouble when he was killed? Dealing dope? Stomping somebody? Doing something he had no business doing?* I didn't ask it, but she read me anyway.

She shrugged. 'He done some time when he was a boy, juvey time right before he turned sixteen. Then a little bit of hard time a long time ago. Nothing big-time.'

'And his name?'

'Shawn. Shawn Raymond.' She said the name tenderly, like

she enjoyed saying it, like she'd probably said it when he was alive, and it all came back to me then: who she was. Who her son was. When and how I'd known them.

Shawn Raymond had been twelve when my brother, Johnny, killed himself. He was a skinny little boy with high cheekbones and eyes as pretty as a girl's. The day of Johnny's funeral, he'd cried as hard as I had: sharp wailing screams that had gone through me like razors. He had stood beside his mother that morning – a thin, homely girl, maybe fifteen years older than me. Bessie. Bessie Raymond.

I'd seen them on and off maybe three or four times before that day. They were both part of a program that Johnny had volunteered for, one of the more progressive things done in the Department when he had been a cop. Project TC, they called it, Touch and Change, and Johnny had caught his share of wisecracks about working with something as warm and fuzzy as that. But my brother had been a hard-assed veteran of 'the wars', as some of the cops called them, good men fighting bad, so when he stepped into the program, lending his support, his name, his goodwill, others had followed.

They had set it up to reach boys without fathers, 'touching and changing' the lives of kids at risk. Each cop was assigned a 'little brother' whom he would 'adopt', taking him around with him for as long as the boy needed it – to ball games, to the malls – helping him out at school and on the block, staying in his corner to stop trouble before it started. It was the kind of thing set up to redeem the name of good cops in a city that saw too many mean ones, something that would earn a photo and a write-up in the *Star-Ledger*.

Shawn Raymond had been Johnny's 'little brother', about eight when they met, a boy who couldn't look you in the face, with toothpick arms, an angular face, and hazel eyes so sad you didn't want to know what they had seen. His face always looked like it needed a wet rag dragged across it, and his hair always needed a trim. Slowly, surely Johnny had brought him around. By the end of their first year, Shawn had put on weight, and muscles, Johnny dragging him to the gym nearly every time he went. By the end of their second, Johnny was buying him clothes, books, a bike, things his young mother never had herself and couldn't dream of getting. By their third year, they were inseparable.

I was in my late teens by then, and all Johnny and I did was fight – about my clothes, my makeup, my boyfriends, 'hoods' in Johnny's estimation. Shawn was young enough to fill the gap I'd left in Johnny's life – his eyes still got wide when Johnny told his tall tales.

My brother's death still touches me daily, and it is never far from the surface. A memory, a word, a bar or two of music, will wash that pain all through me again on any day at any moment. Sometimes it's a voice, sometimes a place, sometimes a name like it was today – Shawn Raymond, who had been as devastated by Johnny's death as I was.

What had happened to Shawn in the years since Johnny's suicide? What had Johnny's violent, self-inflicted death done to a boy standing on the edge of manhood like he had been, a kid who had looked to my brother for his lead? I thought about my own son, Jamal, and what something like that would do to him.

How many times had I passed him on the street and not seen him? Stood beside him in a line with no sense of what we'd shared? I'd put my brother in the ground, dealt with my grief, and never thought again about the others who were grieving, never thought once about the thin boy, or the tough young woman who had been his mother.

I looked again at Bessie Raymond's face, really looked at her this time, not the quick assumptive glance I'd given her before. I lingered on the high-boned cast of her cheeks, the soft lips, the tired, slanted eyes that hid behind the smudged eyeliner. She wasn't in her sixties, how could she be? She was right: the years had changed her good. But I could still see that young woman peeking out – looking the way she'd looked in her twenties. She had come to the house once with Shawn, looking for Johnny – Shawn's mama – all dolled up in a navy dotted-swiss dress with a big pretty collar and short puff sleeves, so different from what I'd expected, so determined to do right by her son, her Shawn, whose name she still said like a prayer. And Johnny was going to help her with him. Until he'd cancelled out any good he ever did. When he left, he must have taken some of her with him too, the way he'd taken some of me, and some of her son – and some of his son too?

'You said Shawn had kids?' I asked her.

'Two boys.'

'Teenagers?'

'The big one is thirteen.'

'What's his name?'

'Rayshawn.'

'Does he look like his father?'

'Like he spit him out not thinking good about it. Why you ask?' Her glance of suspicion and protectiveness told me I'd guessed right.

Without answering her, I stood and walked to the other side of the room and plugged in the kettle. I needed something to do. I didn't want her to see what I knew must be in my eyes, what the memory of that lost time had brought back and what I knew about her dead son . . . and her grandson. But she seemed to know it anyway.

'I don't think either of us got over that man's death,' she said, as much to herself as to me as I stood waiting for the kettle to go off, waiting to gather my thoughts.

What had I known of Bessie Raymond then? What did I know of her now?

The kettle went off and I rummaged through my box of teas, finally settling on something called Tension Tamer (definitely on the money). I dropped it into the cup and splashed in some hot water, spilling some on the table, not bothering to mop it up – one more stain wouldn't matter one way or the other. I let it steep for a moment, and then picked up the cup and sat back down with it, watching the water turn orange from the herbs, avoiding her eyes.

'You know who I am, don't you?' she asked.

'Yes.'

'You remember my boy?'

'Yes, I do.'

'Some son of a bitch killed him, Tamara. Figured he was no good, didn't deserve to live, and I can't live right with that no more. I tried, but I can't live with it no more.' She used the tip of her cigarette to light up another, inhaling it deep and fast, in one breath. I stared down at my tea like I was expecting it to say something, and then sipped, slowly and meditatively.

'He was late twenties, early thirties when he was killed?' I was guessing at Shawn Raymond's age.

'Near thirty.'

'Can you tell me some more about him? What he was doing, who he was seeing. Who his friends were. Was he involved in anything illegal?' I paused after I said that, watching her closely, hating to have to ask it.

She sucked hard on her cigarette, and blew the smoke out above our heads like she was glad to get rid of it. 'He did some dabbling in this and that, but he wasn't no hoodlum or nothing.'

'Dabbling in this and that?'

She glanced sideways, looking at me out of the corner of her eye. 'A man got to make a living. But he was never strung out or nothin' like that. He left that action for his mama.' She added it bitterly, with self-contempt. I had guessed as much from the gaunt hollowness in her eyes and face and the thin hands that she couldn't keep still. I averted my eyes, not wanting to shame her with my gaze.

'I'm clean now,' she added quickly, with a proud lift of her head as she faced me squarely, almost defiantly, showing me she didn't care one way or the other what I thought of her. 'I been lower than the low, but I'm clean now.'

'Could drugs have somehow played a part in your son's death?' I couldn't bring myself to say 'Shawn'. Shawn was twelve and had cried at my brother's funeral. Not a boy gone wrong who had dabbled in this and that, not the father of the hard-edged, high-voiced boy who had held a gun to my heart.

'It wasn't drugs that killed my boy. Not buying them or selling them.'

'Who were his friends?' *More to the point, who weren't his friends?*

'He didn't hang with mens too tough. He had womens, though. My son always did have himself some ladies. He was real popular with the females.' She said it with a grin, as if it were a point of personal pride.

'So he had a lot of women friends?' If they found out about each other, that was definitely enough to get the brother shot.

'Two real ones that I know of. The women did used to like my boy.'

'What were his relationships like with these "real ones"?'

'They was the mamas of his kids.'

20

'Let me get some names and any addresses you have.' I picked up a pen, scribbled her name at the top of a sheet of paper, took down her telephone number and address and then held the pen, poised to jot down the rest.

'Viola Rudell. She the mother of his oldest, Rayshawn. Rayshawn Rudell – Shawn wouldn't give him his name, just being spiteful. They was two of a kind them two, Shawn and Viola, like fire and water – always heating each other up or putting each other out.'

'You said your grandson's name is Rayshawn?'

'Viola named him after Shawn – Shawn Raymond – but turned his names around. That woman is always turning something around. She never meant nobody no good. She ain't no good herself. Ain't never been no good.'

'And the other one? The mother of his other child?'

'Gina. Gina Lennox.' She smiled when she said the girl's name, and her eyes turned soft.

'You liked her, huh?'

'She is a good girl. She comes from a good family. Real good. She could have helped Shawn turn himself around, helped him make himself into somebody.'

'She's the mother of the younger child?'

'My grandbaby. Gus.'

'Gus?'

'She named him after her father, his granddaddy. Augustus Lennox. His full name is Augustus Lennox Raymond. That's a big name for a little baby, ain't it? She lives with her parents far as I know.'

I'd heard, maybe even said the name Augustus Lennox before, but I wasn't sure when or where. I jotted it down, underlining it, and took down Viola Rudell's telephone number and address as well.

'Where did your son live?'

'In the South Ward. In one of them apartment buildings off Avon.'

'And that was the place where his body was found?'

'Yes.'

'And the mothers of his kids?'

'Gina's people live in the South Ward too, over there in one. of them houses on that street with them nice houses on it right off Bergen. Viola live just down the street from me. Off Clinton Avenue.'

'And Rayshawn, the thirteen-year-old, he lives with his mother?'

'He pretty much live where he please. He been in and out of foster care for the last couple of years, but he stay with his mother a lot of the time now. He spends time with me too, when I can get him. He stay over here sometime too. The people he used to live with, the Laytons, live right down the street from this office. That's how I knew you was here. I saw your sign in the window when I was carrying him back to that family.'

'Do you have a picture of Rayshawn?'

She showed me a snapshot of her grandson that confirmed what I already knew. There was something in her eyes when she showed it to me, defiance mixed with pride. I handed it back to her, and she stuffed it back in her wallet, glancing at it again as she tucked it in. 'He's a good-looking boy, ain't he? Look like his granddaddy too, before they got him like they got my son. I don't got one of the other one, the baby,' she added, not waiting for me to ask, her eyes leaving mine as she spoke. 'I ain't seen that baby since he was born. They won't let me nowhere near the child. Nowhere near him.'

'His mother won't let you see him?'

'Her people.'

'Why won't they let you see your grandchild?'

She shrugged offhandedly as if she didn't care, but her answer was in the shame that crossed her face and the voice that shook when she spoke. 'After my boy's daddy died, I wasn't no kind of mama for a while. Doping like I did. Drinking like I used to. I even done some tricking now and again when things got rough. I guess I'll burn in hell for it one day. But that's between me and God, ain't nobody else got nothing to say about it.' She pushed the envelope filled with money across to me, nearly to the edge of the desk.

'When I knew the cops didn't give a damn, you was the only one I could think of to help me because that good man Johnny Hayle was your brother, and he was the only good thing that ever happened in my boy's life. The one who killed him is still out there, eatin', laughin', fartin' on my son's grave.'

'Ms Raymond, I don't know if—'

'Somebody done made him into nothing, like he never was nothing. And you know he was something special, Tamara Hayle, one time long time ago. But he ain't nothin' but a pile of bones now. Nothing.' She muttered it low, her eyes weary with grief, and I realised suddenly with absolute certainty that I owed her because my brother did, and he had always been a man who paid his debts. I reached across my desk and took her thin, rough hands in mine.

'I'll do what I can,' I finally said. 'You've got my word on it.'

Three

About two minutes after Bessie Raymond stepped out of my office I wondered if I'd taken on a lost cause. Bessie had hired me, but Shawn, dead as he was, was truly my client, and a dead client is about as helpful as a dead witness. I knew I should have confronted her about her wannabe thug of a grandson and explained that there was no way in hell I would work for a woman whose grandchild had mugged me in the parking lot.

But I also realised I was tied to this woman – and because of that to her grandson – now that I knew who they were. It was about more than Rayshawn, and even about more than Shawn. It was about my brother, Johnny, and the hole he had left in everybody's life. I knew how much had been taken from Shawn, because I knew how much had been taken from me. It was about that debt that hadn't been paid yet – the one he owed to Bessie's son and grandson, and but for the grace of God, might have owed to my son if I weren't as tough as I am.

Bessie Raymond would never be able to accept the mystery of Shawn's death any more than I could accept the mystery of Johnny's. Her soul wouldn't have any peace, any more than mine could. But finding justice for her dead son just might bring us both a little bit closer to that peace we both needed. So maybe this case wasn't such a lost cause after all.

I should have warned her, though, that I probably wouldn't

have any more luck than the cops had. True, I can sometimes get answers from folks who would rather not talk to cops, and I can slide into spots where they just aren't trusted. But they have means that I don't – namely the legal right to kick somebody's ass.

But I had given the woman my word that I would try, and that was that. So I had another cup of tea – Tension Tamer was taking care of business – and waited for my computer to boot itself up. Then I created a file called YBGB – Young Brother Gone Bad – and jotted down all the names Bessie Raymond had mentioned: Shawn Raymond, Rayshawn and his mother Viola Rudell, Gina and her father Gus Lennox.

I did feel better when I counted the money Bessie had stuffed into the bank envelope. Counting money always has that effect on me. It was more than enough for two weeks' worth of work, more than I'd seen in one lump in a very long time. I also knew it was more than Bessie Raymond would probably ever see again in her life, and that made me sad as hell. I folded it into the pocket of my wallet and shoved it deep inside my bag.

It was half past three; the bank was closed but would open up again around five. I figured it might be wise to go directly to the bank with that kind of cash. I had about an hour and a half to kill, so I turned off my computer, gathered up my things, and headed downstairs to Jan's Beauty Biscuit, the beauty salon on the first floor and one place the cops would never go for answers. It was time for me to start earning Bessie Raymond's life savings, and if there was one person who might have some dirt on the principals involved, it was Wyvetta Green, the Biscuit's owner and chief stylist. I glanced at my nails on the way down the stairs and decided they could definitely do with a coat of polish. You don't plop into Wyvetta Green's chair just to bullshit; she is too much of a businesswoman for that. I pulled twenty bucks from the wad of cash Bessie Raymond had given me and stuck it into my pocket. I also made a mental note to get a receipt so I could list the manicure as a business expense.

Wyvetta Green has owned Jan's Beauty Biscuit for as long as I've known her. Her place is the best thing about this wreck of an office building, and the one thing that gives the place a touch of class. Wyvetta and her gold-toothed boyfriend, Earl, had spared no expense when they renovated the Biscuit a couple of years ago, and the rose-coloured walls, white-and-pink-checked linoleum floors, and cerise faux leather chairs had aged pretty well. They hadn't done such a great job with the exhaust system, though. The scent of chemicals, hair oil, and Lysol spray hit me hard when I stepped through the door.

'Hey, girl, what's up?' Wyvetta said, and I stopped short. She looked like a different person. 'You better check it out fast, 'cause it's off my head tomorrow. I'm straightening this mess into one of them short, sleek cuts, like Jada Pinkett wears. I might dye it blond again too.' I sank into one of the lush chairs and studied Wyvetta's face in the mirror that faced me.

She had cut her hair nearly off, and what was left floated around her face in a soft black halo. I'd never noticed before what a pretty woman Wyvetta was, with her thin, longish face, smooth dark brown skin, and quick, wide smile, which her short haircut now gave its due.

'What you looking at, Tamara?' Her eyes studied me doubtfully.

'Wyvetta, your hair looks good! Besides that, Jada Pinkett is in her early twenties, and she can get away with her hair so short and blond,' I added, forgetting, for a moment, my tact.

'You think this looks good?' She gave the stout, light-skinned woman who had fallen asleep in her chair and to whose reddish

brown hair she applied a white, foaming cream, a slight tug.
The woman sat up, cleared her throat, and began to read the
magazine resting on her plump thighs. 'You okay, Honey?'

'Fine, Wyvetta.' The woman adjusted the horn-rimmed
glasses that had slipped down her nose and tugged at her loose,
polyester blouse.

'Honey, this is Tamara. Tamara, Honey. Tamara Hayle here
is a private investigator, works upstairs. A private investigator
extraordinaire!' The woman nodded respectfully and returned
to her magazine.

'Good?' Wyvetta asked again, fishing for another
compliment.'

'Good. Why are you going to straighten it?'

Wyvetta shrugged. 'I can't be sitting around here looking
good with my hair all cut off.' She peered at me like a teacher
out of patience with a dull student. 'What would it look like
for me, the owner of Jan's Beauty Biscuit, to be sitting around
here with hair cut to my scalp in its natural condition? That's
like Dick Gregory selling Park's pork sausages. It don't make
no kind of sense.'

'But Wyvetta—'

'I'm supposed to be an advertisement for my own product,
Tamara,' she said, with a critical glance at her new hairdo in
the mirror. 'My customers are always coming in here telling
me they want their hair to look like mine. The colour, the cut,
the style. I'm a living commercial for myself!'

I nodded agreeably but had my doubts. I'd seen Wyvetta's
hair go from a lion's mane streaked with gold to a shiny helmet
dusted with silver. She'd been both blond and auburn within
the same week. And once, due to a bad mix of chemicals, dye,
and too much sun, her hair had turned bright red.

'I figured I'd just give my hair a rest,' she continued by way

28

of explanation. 'But I got to straighten this mess out. What would happen to the Biscuit if everybody who came in here started wearing their hair like this? I'd be out of business faster than white on rice.'

'White on rice?' I asked. Wyvetta always got her expressions mixed up. 'Why don't you just add natural-hair care to the things you do? It would be better for your own hair and everybody else's.'

Wyvetta rolled her eyes. 'Ain't no money in it. You can't do nothing with no natural hair. Folks can do it themselves. Why are they going to come out to a hairdresser if all they have to do to look good is wash and dry and comb their own heads? And you can't add colour to natural hair or it ain't natural no more. All I know is, I'm tired of this mess now,' she said. 'Plus Earl likes my hair long.'

'And fake!' added Honey. Both women cackled.

'What can I do for you today, Tamara Hayle?' Wyvetta studied my hair and shook her head in disapproval. 'I wish you'd let me do something with that head of yours, girl. You're a pretty woman, Tamara, and I hope you'll take this in the spirit I give it, but your head just don't do you justice. If you'd let me have some time with it, let me style it for you – add some colour and extensions, throw in some streaks, spark it up some – your hair would take on a life of its own. Don't be scared of colour. Black folks always scared of something. Scared of taking chances!'

'Actually, I came in for my nails.' I extended my hands in her direction.

'Lucy!' Wyvetta yelled. 'Come on out here, baby. You got yourself a customer.'

Lucy, a skinny recent high school graduate who worked for Wyvetta part-time and whom she was grooming to become a stylist, strolled out with a broom in one hand and a fancy straw basket filled with nail polishes in the other. She placed the broom in the closet, pulled over a small table, placed a hand towel over it, and then went to the sink and returned with a cut-glass bowl filled with soapy water. She took my right hand in hers, studied it as if preparing to operate, then placed it in the warm water.

'Want tips?'

'No, just do the best you can with what I've got.'

'You should let me do some tips for you.'

'No thanks. Once you get them, you've got to keep them up, and they always seem to break off the little bit of nail I've got.'

'They do weaken your nails some,' chirped in Honey from Wyvetta's chair.

'It depends on how they're done, and Lucy knows what she's doing because I taught her right,' said Wyvetta, always the business woman.

'If you had the tips I could put something on them, some stars or something,' Lucy said, still hoping.

'No thanks.'

'You sure?'

'You heard the woman say what she wanted, Lucy,' scolded Wyvetta. 'So how's things been going, Tamara? How's Jamal?'

'Fine.'

'Haven't seen him in a while. He's doing okay?'

'Yeah. He's helping a friend fix a computer.'

'Fix a computer! Go on, Jamal with your bad self!' Wyvetta said. 'I just learned how to use a typewriter good.'

'He's really gotten into those computers,' I said, studying the pictures on Wyvetta's wall as if I had nothing else on my mind. After about ten minutes, I got down to the reason for my visit. 'Wyvetta, has a woman named Viola Rudell ever dropped in here for you to do her hair?' I asked in what I hoped was an offhanded way.

'Nope. Never heard of her.'

'You think Tasha might know her?'

'Know who?'

'Viola Rudell.'

'Ask Tasha.'

'How's she doing?' I asked as I made a mental note to give Tasha, Wyvetta's baby sister, a call. She was actually closer in age to Viola Rudell and Shawn Raymond than Wyvetta was, and would probably be a better source of information. 'Is she still living at the same place?'

'Tasha? Yeah. She's still there, but she's not home this week. She went down to Bermuda with some old man she's been seeing. Businessman. She left her boy with me. Earl's daughter, Sandy, is watching him.'

'Bermuda! Where she find herself a man like that? Taking her to Bermuda?' asked Honey, knocking her glasses back up on her nose. 'Whooh! Before I married Harold, the most place a man ever took me was Atlantic City. And I had to pay my own way back.'

'Earl took me to Mexico City a while back when the fares were cheap. He wanted to pay my way down, but I wouldn't let him. He paid for him. I paid for me. That's the way I like it with a man,' Wyvetta added. 'Me and Earl been together a long time, but I don't like to depend on a man too much. Ain't good for me. Ain't good for him.'

We all grunted in agreement. 'But you know Tasha, with her fresh little mouth and them big pretty eyes, she always does seem to tie herself up with some rich old man. Girl seems to have a knack for it,' Wyvetta went on with a disapproving shake of her head.

31

'Yes, she does,' I said, sighing involuntarily as I remembered the last rich old man Tasha Green had tied herself up with. 'Do you know when she'll be back?'

'A couple of days. Week maybe. She just left the day before yesterday.'

Lucy lifted my hand out of the water, dried it off, looked it over again, gently pushed down my cuticles, and filed my nails into ovals with fast, even strokes while my other hand soaked. Then she dried that hand, filed my nails, and prepared to paint. 'You got yourself some pretty hands, Miss Hayle, you should get yourself some tips.'

'Maybe another time.'

'What colour you want?'

'Clear.'

'Clear! I don't know why you even bother, Miss Hayle. You may as well do this yourself.'

'Can't nobody give themselves a good manicure, Lucy,' said Wyvetta, protecting her interests.

Lucy nodded obediently, and then glanced at me. 'You got to let them dry now, Miss Hayle. Don't rub them against nothing. Even though they are clear.'

'Get me that magazine over there, will you, Lucy?' I asked, and she placed an old copy of *Essence* on my lap so I could turn it with the palm of my hand as I held my fingers stiff.

I'd batted zero with Viola Rudell, had three other names to toss out before I left, and Lucy was working fast. I didn't want to drop another name too soon; folks would get suspicious. I believe in keeping a client's confidentiality, and Wyvetta's nose is as good as a hound dog's when it comes to sniffing out something you don't want smelled. If I asked openly about more than one person during the same hour, she was bound to have something to say. You never know where words you speak will end up. So I sat for a while, listening to the others talk, letting my nails dry, going through the pages of the magazine with my palm trying to figure out an angle. Finally it came to me.

'Oooh. I'll bet you all good money that none of you has ever seen a baby as pretty as this one!' I squealed as if finding a picture of a cute baby was all I had on my mind. 'Lucy, hold this picture up so Wyvetta and Honey can see her. I have never seen a baby as sweet as this one!'

It was weak bait, but Honey bit fast.

'You think *that* baby's cute, you should see my grandbaby – I told my daughter she should put that baby in a contest. Wyvetta, hand me my pocketbook.' Possessed by a competitive urge fused with grandmotherly devotion, she dug through her large bag and fished out an expensive-looking leather wallet. With a flourish, she pulled out a dog-eared photo of a nude baby sprawled across a white chenille bedspread, and a chorus of admiring oohs and aahs poured out of everybody's mouth. I studied the photograph carefully, then gave what I hoped sounded like a surprised gasp.

'Well, this is something! This baby looks just like Gina's child. I've never seen a baby look so much like Gina's child.'

'Gina? Gina who?' Honey asked with a scowl.

'Gina Lennox. Are you kin to Gina Lennox, Honey?'

'Gina Lennox? Never heard of her.'

'Maybe your daughter's husband is related to her? Do you know Gina Lennox, Wyvetta? How about you, Lucy? I think she still lives over in the South Ward.' Bessie Raymond hadn't mentioned that she definitely still lived with her parents, so I chanced it.

Wyvetta shrugged. 'I don't think I know her. She hasn't been in here.'

'I don't think she's kin to my son-in-law either,' Honey said,

33

still considering it. Then she slammed the pocketbook down on
her lap and sucked her teeth loudly. 'Lord have mercy, I hope
that boy ain't been fooling around with no other woman! Lord,
I hope that boy ain't had a baby with nobody else. Harold would
have a natural-born Negro fit if he thought that boy had been
messing around on his daughter. He's liable to kill him – make
our child a widow before her time. Ooh, Lord! What did you
say that girl's name was? Here.' She snatched a pen from the
side of the counter. 'Let me write the girl's name down so I
can—'

'No, no, no! I don't think you've got to worry about that.' I
backed down quickly, trying to mend any damage I'd done.
'The father of Gina's child is a man named Shawn Raymond. I
know that for a fact, a definite fact,' I repeated.

'Shawn Raymond? I never heard of him either,' said Wyvetta,
answering my unasked question.

'It's sad what happened to him – Shawn Raymond.' I threw
his name out again, hoping to put an end to any lingering
suspicion Honey had and maybe jar somebody's memory. 'It
was a tragedy. He was murdered a couple of months ago.
Somebody shot him.'

'Shot him!' everyone said in unison.'

'That's what I heard.'

Everybody complained, for the next five or six minutes, about
the number of guns that found their way into the community
and mourned the number of good men who had died because
of it. I didn't mention the fact that Shawn Raymond was
probably not one of them. Then Lucy, who had begun to put
away her things, stopped and stood up straight, as if she'd just
remembered something. 'Gina Lennox?'

'Yeah. Gina Lennox,' I said quickly.

'You mean to tell me that Gina Lennox had a baby?'

34

Pay dirt.

'Yeah, pretty little thing too.' I glanced at my nails, touched one lightly to see if it was dry, blew on them, and then glanced back at the magazine like it didn't matter one way or the other.

'She got married?'

'Not that I know of. She still goes by Lennox.'

'You sure it was Gina, not Lena? It's easy to get them mixed up. Having a baby without a husband sounds like a Lena move to me.'

'Yeah, I'm sure it was Gina,' I said cautiously, knowing by her tone that I was treading on unfamiliar and probably dangerous territory. 'Do they look that much alike?' The look on Lucy's face as she reared back slightly with suspicion in her eyes told me I'd taken a wrong step.

'I thought you said you knew Gina Lennox.'

'Well, I do, but not that well. Her mother is a good friend of a good friend of mine. Actually she knows the father, Shawn Raymond, better. She showed me the picture of their baby.' I figured I could always give her Annie's name if it came to that.

'Gina and Lena Lennox are twins. Identical twins.'

'I always did want to have myself a twin,' Wyvetta commented. 'Earl tells me I got enough passion in me for two women.' Lucy giggled self-consciously, and I filed away this new information on Gina and Lena Lennox, wondering how much if anything it meant and if Bessie Raymond knew about it. It added an interesting twist that might be significant.

Lucy took my hands between hers, rubbing them with a delicious-smelling lotion that reminded me of strawberry shortcake.

'What was that name you said before?' asked Honey. I maintained my look of disinterest, but things were heating up.

'Gina Lennox?'

'No. Before.'

'Shawn Raymond?'

'No, the woman. The other one. Was it Viola Rudell?'

'Yeah. Viola Rudell.'

'That's what I thought you said. Why you want to know about her?'

I paused. 'Someone I know is involved with her,' I said, trotting out a half-truth.

'Tell him to get uninvolved quick. That woman is poison.'

'Poison?' Bessie Raymond had told me that much already. I pushed for more.

'Poison,' Honey repeated solemnly. 'Tell him that unless he wants to leave this life with less than he had coming in, he better leave that heifer right where he found her.'

'What do you mean?'

'Just tell him he should stay as far away from Viola Rudell as clean do from hog. But I ain't going to say nothing else. You know I'm not one to gossip.' She glanced up at Wyvetta with a mischievous wink.

'You got us curious now, Honey, you may as well give up the dirt,' said Wyvetta with a slight yank of the woman's head.

'Ow, Wyvetta. That hurt.'

'You got me interested now.'

'Well, you know, Wyvetta, I don't like to be gossiping about anybody.'

Wyvetta rolled her eyes. 'Go on and say what you want to say, Honey.'

'You know my daughter Belinda, who has that pretty baby I just showed you all? Well, her best friend, a girl named Lydia, got into a fight with that Viola Rudell. You remember Lydia, Wyvetta, she was supposed to be coming into the Biscuit for

you to style her hair. I don't know if you ever saw her or not –
it was a while ago when I told her.'

'Lydia? Was that the girl—'

'Yeah, that was her.' Honey cut her off, her tone hushed.
'She got that scar running down the side of her face like that
from Viola Rudell.'

'Viola Rudell was the one who cut that girl up like that?'

'Yes, so now you know why I'm talking like I'm talking,'
Honey said with a glance toward me. 'She was such a pretty
girl. She'd just gotten out of high school, heading down South
to college, not too much older than Lucy here, and she and
Viola Rudell got into it over some man, and that bitch – and
you know I don't use that word lightly – that bitch cut the
girl's face like that. Like to killed Lydia's mother to see her
child's face all cut up. Lydia comes from a good family too. I
don't know what she was doing messing around with a man
who would have something to do with a woman like Viola
Rudell!

'They tried to get all kind of plastic surgery to fix the girl's
face, must have cost somebody some money, but I think her
family had it to spare, if you know what I mean. But you know
black folks' skin will keloid on them, and that's what happened
to that girl's face. She's got that keloid scar running down the
edge of her face like a rope. I remembered Viola Rudell's name
because it sounds like "violence". That's why it stuck in my
mind.'

Wyvetta laid down her comb and we were all silent for a
moment, out of respect for this girl whom none of us knew but
whose tragedy touched us.

'I remember her now,' Wyvetta said quietly. 'She did come
in here once, and I tried to style her the best I could. That scar
ran right down the side of her face. Right down the side.'

'Why would Viola Rudell cut her like that?' asked Lucy.

'Evil,' snorted Honey.

'A lot of people are evil, but that don't mean they got to cut somebody's face,' Lucy said.

'Especially over some no-good man that didn't mean neither of them no good,' added Honey.

I wondered who that no-good man had been.

'Women do some crazy things over men,' said Wyvetta with a solemn nod of her head. 'And most of 'em ain't worth it.'

Honey nodded in agreement. 'I love Harold, and I'd do most anything for him, but I'll be damned if I'd cut up some woman's face over him.'

'I ain't ever known any man worth fighting over,' said Wyvetta, picking up the comb again. 'Not even Earl. Any man who's worth anything don't want some crazy woman fighting over him, anyway.'

'But some of them likes it. You know that as well as me,' added Honey. 'Makes them feel important. Like you get a lot of silly women who like men fighting over them.'

'I don't know any man who would ever fight over me, and I don't know any man I would ever fight over. I don't even know any men. All I know is little boys,' said Lucy, turning the mood light, and we all laughed, glad to be talking about something else.

'That's what most of them are, anyway. Little boys, looking for a Big Mama to take care of them. I love Earl like the dickens, but if the truth be told, he can be just as young and silly as the rest of them.'

'I don't know what Harold would do without me,' said Honey.

'More than you think!' Wyvetta quipped. 'Tamara, I know you got something to say on this subject. You ever hear from

38

what's his name? Last thing I heard—'

I threw her an evil look, and she closed her mouth. My love life – what little there was of it – was not for public consumption. But the last thing Wyvetta had heard was pretty good. I'd spent a hot night in a warm place with a brother as refreshing as cool, sweet drink. But that had been a while ago. And there had been nobody since. When it came to men, times were hard, and I'm a hard woman to please. Maybe too hard sometimes, which could be the root of my problem. But things do get lonesome out here, and sometimes I feel down about it. With her keen sense of reading folks, which made her one of the most popular beauticians in Essex County, nobody knew that better about me than Wyvetta Green.

'You're a good woman, Tamara Hayle,' she said, sensing in my glance my self-doubt. 'Something good will come your way. You got too much to offer a good man to be sitting around here by yourself.'

'Um, hum,' Honey hummed in agreement.

'Ain't nobody smarter than you are, and you're pretty too. Be prettier if you'd let me do something with them naps. Plus you got your own business – and that's something, believe me. And you have a son. A lot of women out here wish they had a child to help them chase away the blues,' Wyvetta added, surprisingly wistful. 'You just got to meet a man who's up to your standards. And I got to tell you, girl, I don't know about that last one you was with. You know who I'm talking about.'

I'd made the mistake of telling Wyvetta more about my business – and that refreshing, cool drink in the warm place – than I should have. She'd been glad for me but hadn't entirely approved. In Wyvetta Green's book, lust ran a distant second to loot as far as men went. 'You need to find yourself a businessman. Somebody like yourself. Somebody who can offer

you something besides a . . . a good time.' She glanced at the
other women and chose her words tactfully.

'Ain't nothin' wrong with a good time!' Honey chuckled,
reading between the lines. 'I wish I'd had myself a few more
good times when I had the chance.'

'Ain't nothing stopping you from having a good time now,
Honey,' said Wyvetta.

''Cept Harold and his .22. But there's good times and there's
good times.'

'Got that straight.' I threw in my two cents, remembering
my hot night with that cool, sweet drink.

'A good time will keep your feet warm in half-dollar socks,'
said Wyvetta.

'Make you smack your mama square in her mouth!' tossed
in Honey.

'I ain't never had no good time as good as that!' Lucy said,
her eyes big with wonder, and we all fell out laughing,
reminiscing and swapping those tales we were comfortable
sharing. And after a while, glad I'd gotten what I came for, I
took my receipt, said my goodbyes, and headed to the bank to
deposit my money.

Four

Jake was walking to his car as I drove into my driveway, and my heart skipped a beat. As usual. It doesn't embarrass me anymore, even though it probably should – lusting after a married man like that. But my feelings for him have become one of those things I've grown to accept about myself – like that extra five pounds that cling to my behind.

It's one thing to take a sip of a sweet, cool drink like I had that hot night in Jamaica, but you need more than a sip to keep you going. I don't have a hell of a lot of luck with men. They're either leaving me, lying to me, or dying. Except for two, that is – my son Jamal and Jake Richards. The problem is that Jake, a something-good kind of man if there ever was one, belongs to somebody else.

I've known him nearly all my life. He was one of the young brothers hanging on to what passed as my brother's wisdom when they played ball in our dustbin of a backyard a cough and a wink from Newark. He has been there for me when I was too scared or stubborn to ask for help from anybody else, which is most of the time. He was my first big crush, one of the best-looking guys that came around. And he's still fine. Rock-your-boat-drop-your-panties fine, which seems to deepen despite each grey hair and each trace of sadness that comes into his eyes.

He is more assured these days than he used to be, easy with

the acclaim that comes from being one of the best public defenders in Essex County. But he is still the humble guy he's always been, there for anybody who needs him – from the scared, wild teenager looking for help to the widow lady who needs a ride to church. Half the time it's me or Jamal.

Jake had on his work clothes tonight, the whole take-care-of-business lawyer package, and he looked good. But he always looks good, be it dashing around the ball court in the red gym shorts that cling like satin or strolling into the courtroom in his pin-striped suit and wing-tipped shoes. He has a natural elegance about him – Duke Ellington grace, my daddy used to call it.

His eyes lit up as I walked toward him.

'Just dropped Jamal off. He was playing around with one of those old Apples I brought home from the job. Don't tell him I told you, but I think he's trying to fix up one for you as a surprise. I took him by Red Lobster for some shrimp as a reward,' he added in a confidential tone.

'I know he loved that.'

'Late night, huh?'

'I dropped by the bank and stopped by the Pathmark. Jamal will bring them in,' I added as he glanced toward my car, preparing to help me with the bags I'd left there.

'The bank? Hey, that sounds like good news!'

'Depends on how you look at it.'

He glanced at me, concern coming into his eyes. 'So, what's going on?'

'Nothing.'

'You sure about that?'

'No.'

'If you feel like talking about it, I've got some time. Denice is babysitting, and Phyllis—' He stopped short. I didn't push it.

'Sure. Come on in.'

Jamal bounded downstairs as we walked in. He still runs to greet me, even though those size 12s pounding like they do rock the house these days. Every morning he seems to wake up a good two inches taller than when he went to bed, and he's filling out in the shoulders and chest in a way that makes teenage girls – and some grown women, I'm sad to say – do a double take. He's handsome like my brother and father were, and I can see bits of both of them in him when I least expect to see them. I just gaze at him sometimes in wonder. When he saw Jake, a mysterious smile spread on his face, right below the fuzz on his upper lip he's so proud of.

'Can't seem to pull yourself away, can you, man? Just what are your intentions, honorable or otherwise, toward my mother?' His question had a teasing edge but also a tinge of hostility to it that made my mouth drop open in surprise. Jake was taken aback too. But he recovered quickly.

'Your mother and I are friends, man, you know that. Now go get the stuff out her car for her, and stop trying to talk about what you don't know about,' he answered with a firm playfulness that put Jamal in his place. Jamal smiled as if he had put something over on somebody and headed out to the car. Jake glanced at me and shook his head.

'Let's not take it there, but I guess I've got to talk to the boy,' he said in a low voice, thinking maybe what I was thinking. I nodded, continuing our mutual, unspoken agreement not to acknowledge the feelings that we probably share. Or maybe we don't.

You can't keep a damn thing from a kid, especially one as sharp as my son, so I make it a practice not to keep secrets from him. But we've never talked about my feelings toward Jake, even though Jamal can look at my face and know immediately whatever I'm trying to hide, be it fear, exhaustion, or those urges that threaten to overwhelm my better judgment.

Jamal is my only child – going to *be* my only child – and we hens with one chick have our own special link to our offspring, which comes from raising a kid by yourself with no bucks, support, or peace most of the time. It's a bond of protectiveness, loyalty, and occasional sick-to-death-of-each-otherness that's different from the ties that bind other mothers to their children. I wish my son weren't so smart about me, that I could fool him more often than I can. I wish it for his good as much as my own.

Because Jamal has a nosy kid's instinct about my love life and lack thereof, it wouldn't surprise me at all if he'd sensed my attraction to Jake. It wouldn't even surprise me if he'd confronted Jake (the way sons will do when they try to get into your business) about what he called his 'intentions', warning him not to take advantage of me, even though I know he loves and respects Jake as much as I do. I also know that Jake would answer him truthfully no matter what his response was, and that neither of them – in their own particular style of male bonding – would ever share the details of that conversation with me, even if I asked them.

So I didn't 'take it there,' as Jake suggested. The truth was, I really didn't want to deal with what taking it there might mean for me and Jake – or for me and Jamal. Some conversations are better never spoken.

I'd opened a bottle of Merlot when Annie had dropped by earlier in the week, hoping to show me the slides from her ten-day cruise in the Caribbean. I hadn't been in the mood for her tales of sunning and funning with her loving spouse and sorors on a luxury ship in the Caribbean, and sensing that, she wisely hadn't told any. We'd ended up stuffing ourselves on leftover pizza and sipping wine instead. There was still enough left in the bottle for two glasses, so I poured Jake and myself a glass. We sipped for a moment, facing each other across my old Formica table, listening to the hum of the refrigerator and Jamal hustling with the grocery bags on the back porch.

My kitchen is full of memories – of my family, my son's early days, and all those lonesome breakfasts and dinners. Every year I plan to paint it, put in a new floor, refinish the cabinets to give it some style, but every year my hopes run straight up against the reality of my pocketbook, so it looks pretty much as it did when my family first moved in. But it gets nice sun in the morning, which brightens up the faded flowered wallpaper and pale yellow counters, even though at night the fluorescent globe highlights every grease spot and smudge mark ol' Mr Clean can't seem to touch. Sitting across from Jake this evening, I realised that there was nothing even remotely romantic about the room. That was probably a good thing.

'Where do you want them, Ma?' Jamal asked, breaking the silence as he burst into the kitchen through the back door with two bags in each hand. It was growing colder, and a blast of chilly air and dead leaves followed him in.

'That's fine.' I nodded toward a space halfway between the refrigerator and the pantry and he dropped the bags. The phone rang and he jumped to get it, assuming it was for him, which it was. He put the phone on hold and, without looking back, dashed out of the room to take it on the extension in his room.

'Busy guy,' Jake commented with a nod.

'Too busy.'

'Remember those days when all you had to think about was yourself?' He spoke wistfully, almost sadly.

'I don't *want* to remember those days,' I said, and we both laughed, me with a shudder as I recalled the crazy days of my youth, the sparkle in his eyes reminding me just how much of that past we shared. When he shifted in his chair, I noticed that his suspenders were the ones I'd helped his daughter Denice pick out for Father's Day last year. Phyllis had gone into the hospital that week, a bad reaction to an overdose of medication. He had been through hell, and the gift had been as much from me as from his kid.

Jake has been married as long as I've been Jamal's mother, which seems like all my adult life. We were friends once, Phyllis and me, although she's a few years older. She was a sweet, fragile girl who grew up to be a frightened, haunted woman. After the birth of Denice, she started having her spells. That's what Jake calls her fits of rage, with a sad familiarity and humour that tells me they are woven into him as deeply as Johnny's suicide is into me. Some of Phyllis's days are good ones, but then there are the others when she won't take the pills that smooth things out and give her some peace.

She had not taken them for four days running before that Father's Day, and then gobbled them all down at once and ended up in the hospital, her body jerking in spasms, her mouth wide with silent screams. I'd taken Denice shopping the next morning, buying her anything she wanted, and adding thirty bucks to the ten she'd saved so she could buy her father something for Father's Day that she knew he'd never buy for himself. His voice had caught when he called me that night to thank me.

'So what's going on with you?' I asked now, wondering if he'd thought about me when he put those suspenders on this morning. He took a sip of wine, and gave me a tired, melancholy smile that told me that what he was wearing had probably been the farthest thing from his mind.

'About the same,' he answered me in a low voice, with a finality that said his wife was probably back in the hospital

and he didn't want to talk about it. I accepted that, not taking
him anywhere he didn't want to go.

Let's not take it there.

I took another sip of wine, and then went over to the bags
that Jamal had piled on the floor and methodically began to
put things away, disturbed by the feelings I couldn't express
and annoyed about how little food you get for the amount of
money you pay. I was saddened too about the money in that
envelope Bessie Raymond had given me. When I'd gotten to
the bank and actually counted the cash, it had been mostly tens
and ones – her life savings maybe, but not enough for more
than three weeks at most. I felt guilty about the bite it had
taken out of her, and how little she might end up getting for it.
She had given me everything she had to find out who had killed
her son, and in the end the most it would buy would be maybe
a month or so of groceries. What the hell kind of shameful
thing was that?

'You ever hear of a guy named Shawn Raymond?' I asked
Jake when I sat back down. 'He was killed a few months ago.
He opened the door of his apartment and somebody blew him
away, according to his mother.'

'Happened a few months ago?'

'April twenty-fifth.'

'Vaguely.'

'Happened somewhere over in the South Ward.'

'Hmph.'

'What does "Hmph" mean?'

'Just thinking about the South Ward.'

'What about the South Ward?'

'That's where I always wanted to live when I was a kid.
You don't remember it in its heyday, do you?'

'It must not be the same place it is now.' A part of the city

47

that had spawned the likes of Shawn Raymond and Viola Rudell didn't seem like a place Jake would aspire to live.

'I remember Clinton Avenue when I was a kid. My daddy used to take me over there on Saturday mornings, like I take Denice to Fifth Avenue in New York. It had those wide, old boulevard streets, proud and pretty. All you wanted to do when you were a kid was grow up and own one of those houses on one of those streets.' He reminisced with his voice more melancholy than I'd ever remembered hearing it. I put down my glass and listened, wondering about the change, and if it was just the South Ward's past and present he was talking about.

'There were fancy stores then, furriers, jewellers. You could buy a ring on Clinton Avenue as good as you could get in Tiffany's.'

'Things have changed.'

'I walk through those streets now and the only words that come out my mouth are "used to be": "This used to be . . . That used to be . . ." Denice thinks I'm lying to her when I tell her how things used to look.'

'It was the riot?'

'That's what they like to blame. The city has always been corrupt. Politicians were robbing this city blind before the first brick was ever thrown. Newark is like some crazy old lady giving her jewels away to the first dude she meets with flashing eyes and fast hands. The riot was nothing but the last straw. Whites not wanting to live near black folks, anywhere near black folks. And black folks sick and tired of a racist city hall that ignored their neighborhoods, and cops who beat their sons and brothers and husbands for no good reason at all.'

'The riot started over some cop killing a kid, didn't it?'

'That was the rumour, anyway. But that's how it always

48

starts, isn't it, over some stupid cop shooting somebody's kid? The white folks left the city overnight it seemed, taking the tax base and what was left of the money with them. And all the places you could take your kid to for a milk shake on a Saturday afternoon disappeared.'

'All I remember about the riots was how my eyes burned from the smoke, and how my grandma rocked back and forth like she was in a trance when the national guardsmen swore they saw a looter in the apartment downstairs and let loose a round of ammo in the building. They killed a lady, a pregnant lady, pulled forty some bullets out of her.' I felt the old bitterness creep into my voice, like the memory of the tickle of the tear gas in the back of my throat. If I thought hard enough about it, I could taste it, even now. 'They kept Johnny overnight in jail. Said he didn't have proper identification to be walking down the street. That and the way they killed that pregnant woman drove my grandma to her bed.'

'A lot more people died in that riot than the papers wanted to say, killed by nervous white suburban kids who had never seen a black person up close and personal before in their lives. The city was in an honest-to-God state of siege. There was them and there was us, and that changed everything and everybody forever,' Jake said.

'We left soon after that. I don't think it was because of the riots, I think Daddy had just saved enough money to finally get us out of the projects, and this place looked like a palace then.' I glanced around the kitchen with an amused smile as I remembered that first night in this kitchen. I'd thought we were rich.

'It would still look like a palace to a lot of kids,' Jake said. 'A lot of people left Newark, like your folks did. Mine did too, a couple of years later. But not everybody. Some moved into those pretty houses in the South Ward where they couldn't live before, taking a stab at that dream. But the spec guys were there by then too, smelling big money, selling to absentee landlords who would rent to the first fool they could find and then burn the place down for the insurance money. There were days when the whole damn city was lit up like a birthday cake, and everybody pretended not to know how the fires started. Whole blocks burned, and those fires were seed money for fortunes planted back then – and none of those seeds seemed to root themselves in Newark.

'Banks started redlining, and before you knew it, people whose only dream was making it to the next morning started moving in. But some people stayed, rearing their kids, watching their property values slide into the toilet, cursing to themselves as the local drug dealer plied his trade in the house next door. And then came crack – a poor man's version of a rich man's drug. A couple of years and a city's soul was gone.' He shrugged his shoulders and then chuckled self-consciously. 'Wonder where all that came from? Didn't mean to go into a sociopolitical rant on you. Urban Decay 101 as defined by Jake E. Richards,' he added with a little bow.

'Anytime you want to preach, you got a choir.'

He held up the glass of wine and studied it, half joking. 'Maybe I better stop drinking this stuff if a couple of sips will do that to me. What did you say the dude's name was?'

'Shawn Raymond. His family was one of those whose only dream was making it to the next morning,' I said, and told him about Bessie Raymond, what she had told me about her son's death, and how she was convinced that the cops didn't care and that I could help her out. 'I doubt if I'll get anything, but if I do I'll turn it over to the cops who are handling the case.'

Jake thought for a minute. 'Do you know who handled it?'

'You think you can find out for me?'

'I'll check around.' He thought for another moment. 'Obviously Shawn Raymond knew whoever killed him, because he let him or her in his house.'

'Obviously.'

'What did he do for a living?'

'Small-time hustler, probably. I got the feeling from his mother that he wasn't exactly an upstanding citizen, even though she swore he didn't deal drugs.' I left out what I knew about Rayshawn and the parking lot. Jake would go into his big-brother mode, and I didn't feel like hearing his mouth about the chances I take or the hours I keep. 'And she's probably right about the cops. They probably didn't give a damn because they'd seen him before and knew he didn't mind doing somebody dirty.'

'They may have figured he had it coming. Gangsters killing gangsters.'

'Niggers killing niggers,' I quoted Bessie Raymond.

'I wouldn't go that far. Cops are people like everybody else. Some good, some bad – you know that. If it comes down to putting in some extra time finding the bullet that snuffed out somebody's college-bound kid or the one that took out some small-time hoodlum, you know which bullet they'll look for first. You can't blame them.'

'So where does that leave Bessie Raymond?'

'Coming to you for help. How old a guy was he?'

'Near thirty.'

'Damn shame. Do you have any sense of him, what kind of people he hung with? Where he partied?'

'I'm going to stop by his mother's place sometime tomorrow. When I go through his things, I'll get a better sense of him.'

'Did you get any names from her?'

'A couple. You sure you want to know all this?' *Am I sure I want to tell you?* Jake has good instincts, and his memory for details is phenomenal, but I wasn't sure I had the right to tell him everything, or if it was a breach of confidence. But on the other hand, a lot of names come across his desk, and he might know something that would help me out.

'Viola Rudell? Ever heard of her?' I finally asked. Maybe she'd slashed somebody else with her blade. 'She's supposed to be violent, very violent. She carved up some girl's face.'

'Jesus.' Jake shuddered. 'Over the same dude who got killed? If he was tipping on her again, maybe she got wise and decided to do him in this time.'

'Could have been.'

'Watch yourself when you talk to her.'

'You don't have to worry about that. Ever heard of Gina Lennox? Lena Lennox?'

'Doesn't ring a bell. South Ward again?'

'Probably. Twins. The family lives on a side street off Bergen.'

A light came into his eyes. 'You're not talking about Gus Lennox's daughters, are you?'

'Gus Lennox, as in Augustus Lennox?'

'He goes by Gus. He always used to say Augustus made him sound like some Roman emperor.'

'I thought that name sounded familiar.'

'Gus Lennox.' Jake repeated the name softly and deferentially. 'How's he doing?'

'I have no idea. His name was just one of those Bessie Raymond threw out.'

'What do you mean threw out?'

'Just what I said, she threw his name out.'

'I know you don't think Gus Lennox is mixed up in this mess?'

'His daughter's boyfriend was killed. It could have been—'

'Tamara, don't put Gus Lennox's good name in the middle of something like that. Unless you have some kind of seriously smoking gun, you don't want to involve his family—'

'What the hell are you talking about, Jake?' I cut him off, annoyed with myself for forgetting my professional ethics and telling him the man's name in the first place. 'Gus Lennox, Augustus Lennox, is already in the middle of it. His daughter's boyfriend was murdered. Not only that, but he's standing in the way of Bessie Raymond seeing her grandbaby. That's what Bessie Raymond says, anyway.'

'He probably has a good reason for making that decision.'

'Good reason? Who the hell does he think he is? God?' I shot back, thinking about the hurt in Bessie Raymond's eyes.

'I know and respect Gus Lennox. He's fought the good fight for as long as there was one to fight. Ever hear of the Prince Street Gang in the late fifties, early sixties? They made the Latin Kings, the Crips, the Bloods, and the rest of these gangbangers carrying on today look like Brownies. These guys were r-o-u-g-h – rough! Heroin, numbers, prostitution, extortion – if it made money and looked like dirt, these dudes were into it.

'Gus Lennox came on the force a rookie cop, went undercover – the first black cop to go undercover – and made his bones getting all the dope there was to get on them. The white boys didn't give a damn about Prince Street and what those hoodlums were doing to the lives of the families who lived there, but Gus did, and he wasn't going to stand for it. Ended up taking one guy out before it was over. To this day, nobody really knows how he was able to infiltrate that gang the way he did. Later on, he blew the whistle on so many corrupt, racist white cops, to this day it amazes me that he

lived to retire. He paved the way for everybody else, Tamara.'
He slammed his glass down on the table for emphasis.

Neither of us said anything for a minute. Jake and I rarely
disagree, and I wasn't sure what to make of this defense of
Gus Lennox. I also wasn't sure if I wanted to share anything
else about my case with him.

Jake broke the silence, his tone softening. 'I was talking
earlier about those families in the South Ward that stayed when
everybody else pulled out. Gus Lennox was one of those
brothers, not letting nothing drive him out of that piece of plot
he'd claimed. He held on to it. He never walked away from
this city, and I have a lot of respect for the dude. He not only
talks that talk, he walks that walk.' He drained his glass as if
toasting Gus Lennox's tenacity.

'So you think Gus Lennox killed Shawn Raymond because
he didn't want him fooling around with his daughter?' I asked,
only half joking.

'Hey, where'd you get all that?' Jake held up his hands in
self-defense, laughter suddenly in his voice.

'You're talking like a defense attorney, and wherever there's
a defense attorney there's somebody who needs a defense.'

'There are half a dozen guys in the criminal justice system
– on both sides of the aisle, I might add – who would defend
Gus Lennox for no other reason than they don't like to hear his
name sullied. I'm surprised you don't remember him. I know
Johnny—'

'I didn't say I didn't remember him,' I said quickly. 'As a
matter of fact, I remember Gus Lennox very well.' That wasn't
the whole truth. When Bessie Raymond mentioned the name, I
hadn't remembered, but now, in the context of the police force,
I recalled. But the Lennox I really remembered was Gus's little
brother, Ben.

Ben Lennox had played quarterback for his high school team. He'd been smart, upstanding, reasonably good-looking, the kind of young man every mother – or big brother – dreams of for her teenager. The kind of boy any teenage girl with sense would have wanted for herself. But not me, the young Tamara Hayle. I found Ben Lennox with his good grades, good manners, and good behaviour as boring as a bowl of cold oatmeal. Nice boy going places? Not for me – not in those days, anyway. Give me that fast-talking, slow-moving little hood who'd end up in the joint.

Ben – probably to shut his brother's mouth, now that I think about it – had asked me to his junior prom, and I had gone with him, to shut my own brother up. And we'd actually had a good time, although I got hot ever time the boy I really liked, Randy, with his good-looking, smooth-talking self, had slow-danced by with the tarty cheerleader who had invited him. Yet I'd had a good time with Ben Lennox, talking easily with him and giggling at his jokes (due mostly to the grass I'd smoked in the backyard with one of my girlfriends before he picked me up).

Ben Lennox had gone to a boarding school out of the state for his last year in high school, and then to college, and I hadn't seen him again until right after my divorce. I was ready by then for a boring good brother who could help me raise my son. We had gone out five or six times before I finally slept with him. I'm not sure why, except I liked him and I knew he liked me and I thought it could turn into something, which it didn't. He'd sent me some roses, called me once or twice and promised he'd see me again. I waited, disgusted with myself for being played for a fool and caring so much. The next thing I heard, he was married. A rueful, sadder-but-wiser smile crossed my lips now as I thought about Ben Lennox, and I dropped my head slightly so Jake wouldn't see it, which he did anyway.

'Didn't you and his brother – what was his name, Jim, Tim? – have something going after you left DeWayne?'

'It was Ben, and we went to the prom when we were kids, had dinner a couple of times after that, and that was it. What do you know about Gina and Lena Lennox?' I changed the subject quickly.

'Not much. Which one was involved with your boy?'

'Gina.'

'Good-looking young girls. Pretty,' Jake added as an afterthought. 'One was kind of wild as I remember it, got into a little trouble. He is very protective of them. You know that father-daughter thing.' He gave a self-conscious chuckle, and I knew he was thinking of Denice.

'Gus Lennox will probably be my first stop after Bessie Raymond,' I said, as much to myself as to Jake, wondering about Gus Lennox and Ben. Funny how after all this time, they all were coming back into my life: Bessie Raymond. Shawn Raymond. Gus Lennox. Ben.'

Jake glanced at his watch. 'About that time, I guess.' He stood, and I rose to walk him to the door.

'So what's going on, Jake?' I asked him on the way out. It was safe now. He was going home. He could share what he wanted to share and end it when he wanted to, but that familiar sorrow came back into his eyes.

'She went back in . . . for a while.'

'What can I do?'

He threw me a look of gratitude that told me what I already knew. 'What you always do, Tam. Just be there for Denice . . . for me.' He paused before he spoke again, focusing his eyes away from mine, on the wall just above the door. 'When it's good, it's the best I could ever hope for, and I don't regret any of it. There's no way in hell the woman she was – is – was – wouldn't have been there for me if it had come down on me like it has on her. This whole thing is the hardest thing I've ever dealt with in my life. But I love her and everything she is, has been, and will ever be, and I can't do anything to change that. It's as simple as that.'

He kissed my forehead then, his scent and nearness going straight through me, and walked to his car, his head bent slightly. I watched him go, wondering if ever in my life I'd find a man who would love me the way he did her.

Five

Jake had it right about Gus Lennox's neighbourhood. It was an oasis of middle-class stability in a desert of urban despair. I'd called Jake to get the address, and parked a block down from the house, not yet ready to question Lennox or his family. The house was a large red brick colonial with the same well-kept veneer of the houses that surrounded it, all separated by ancient trees and neatly trimmed bushes. Several men in sweat suits raked leaves and an elderly woman swept dirt off her front stoop with a vengeance. It was the same Saturday morning ritual you'd see in any suburban neighborhood in the state, and a marked contrast to the street only a few blocks away on which earlier I'd found Bessie Raymond's small apartment.

Bessie had asked me to drop by in the morning because she worked in a hotel nights and slept most of the day. There were still traces of curlicued trim and gargoyles gracing the entrance of her once grand building, which stood next to a stately professional building that now housed members of the world's oldest. The building stood on the crest of a hill from where I could see the grey spiky shadows of the New York City skyline. Somebody had once paid very big bucks to be greeted by that view every morning. I thought about Jake and understood his profound sense of loss for this city he loved.

A kid's voice brought me back. 'You from the County? You

look like you're from the County.'

She was about six and sitting in the shadow of a partially opened door. I wouldn't have noticed her if she hadn't said anything. Her hair was braided in intricate, glossy cornrows dotted with yellow beads, and her face looked like somebody had done some serious overtime with a bottle of Jergens lotion. She wore a lightweight, frilly skirt, more suited for spring than fall, a Pocahontas T-shirt, and lacy anklets that had sunk down into mismatched Mary Janes. A chocolate-brown Barbie knockoff was wedged between her bony knees, and she held a small pink brush.

'No, I'm just here to visit somebody,' I said as I knelt down to her level. 'I'm here to see Ms Raymond.' I wondered if her mother, who from the look of that head obviously cared, had warned her about talking to strangers. Like most kids, she probably forgot it the moment she stepped out the house. 'Do you know where Ms Raymond lives?' Bessie had given me the address but not the number of her apartment.

'You here because of Shawn, aren't you? You going to find out who whacked him?' she asked dramatically, her eyes big.

'I don't know.' I've never been good at lying to kids. 'What's your name, baby?'

'Pandora. What's yours?' She brushed her doll's hair with firm, even strokes, the way somebody probably brushed hers.

'Tamara Hayle. I'm a private investigator.'

'A private investigator! Like on TV?'

'Like on TV. Does your mother know where you are?'

'She's at work.'

'Who's watching you?'

'My brother.' She rolled her eyes and nodded toward a barred, open window on the first floor through which I could see the head of a boy about thirteen sitting in front of a TV set.

60

'Pandora, don't you be talking to nobody!' he yelled through the bars.

'Mind your own business, fool,' Pandora yelled back, and gave me a sly smile. 'What you going to ask Ms Raymond?'

'About Shawn. Did you know him?'

'Kind of. Ms Raymond lives next door to me. Sometimes she watches me when my brother can't. Shawn used to come by.'

'Was he nice?' Kids, dependent upon the goodwill of adults, sometimes have a pretty good sense of people. Pandora cocked her head as if she were seriously considering my question.

'Kind of.'

'Kind of what?'

'He gave me ten dollars once.'

'Ten dollars? That's more than "kind of" nice!'

She laughed a deep, hearty laugh that hinted at the sense of humour she'd have when she grew up. 'I earned that money!'

'Earned it? How?'

'Did a job for him.'

'What kind of job did he have you doing?' Concerned, I sat down on the porch beside her.

'Don't tell my mama.'

'I won't tell anybody. What did Shawn have you do?'

'Looking out.'

'Looking out for what?'

'For Chee-chee.'

'Chee-chee?'

She shrugged and continued. 'He told me to tell him when Chee-chee came.'

'What did Chee-chee look like?'

'You better stop talking to that lady, Pandora, before I tell Mama!' Pandora jumped as her brother's voice boomed from

61

the window. 'You better come on in this house. Don't make me
have to come out there and get you!'

'You ain't coming out here to get nobody, fool!'

'Who you calling fool, girl?'

'Who you think?' Pandora glanced back at the window,
shook her head like a wise old woman, and then stuck out her
tongue in the direction of her brother. We both stood up as she
headed inside.

'Thank you for helping me, Pandora. I really appreciate it.
But can you answer one more question?'

'Like on TV?'

I held the door open for her, a bit ashamed to have to pump
a child for information. 'Yeah, a little like TV. What did Chee-
chee look like?'

She shrugged. 'Like Shawn's friend,' she said as her brother
opened the apartment door, snatched her inside, and tossed me
a dirty look before I could introduce myself. As I rang the bell
next door, I made a mental note to ask Bessie to explain to the
child's mother who I was if it should come up, but I doubted
that it would.

I had a name, though, and that was more than I had coming
in.

Chee-chee. I had assumed it was a man, but it could have
been a woman – that name could belong to either one, and a
six-year-old's interpretation of a 'friend' could mean anything
from a girlfriend to somebody who showed up every now and
then looking for a drink.

Chee-chee.

The walls outside Bessie Raymond's apartment were about
the same sorry shade as my office – grayish brown – and every
fourth tile was missing from the elaborate triangular pattern in
front of her door. The bell looked like it was broken, so I rang

it twice and was poised to ring it again when she answered, dressed in a yellow version of the lime-green uniform she'd had on before.

'Come on in. I been going through his things again. I'll show you where they's at.' She deliberately avoided my eyes, and I realised she had been crying. She led me into a very long, narrow corridor lit with a dim light bulb, which led into an oddly shaped living room. The room smelled like cigarette butts and burned pork. There was a small, black fake leather couch against the wall, two matching TV tables, and a large colour TV sitting against another wall on a wooden bookcase. An oversized, elaborate silver frame containing an old photograph of a man in his mid- or early twenties sat on top of the TV. The man was young and bare-chested, his pants slung low around his trim waist. A cigarette dangled in his mouth and he held a toddler, about the same age as baby Gus.

A partially eaten breakfast of scrambled eggs, toast, and sausages sat on a chipped plate on one of the tables. Except for a calendar flipped to the month of April, the month her son died, the walls were bare. A large, open suitcase and several cardboard boxes were piled in a corner. She glanced at the pile and shook her head.

'That's all that's left of him. His landlord got rid of his bed, dresser, and couch. That there is his TV. I gave the stereo to Rayshawn along with the other good stuff. His clothes, some gold jewellery, anything that looked like it might be worth something. I just hope that damn Viola Rudell don't get her hands on nothing. I don't know what that little baby is going to do, not getting nothing from his daddy 'cept his name.' She shook her head in what looked like exasperation. 'I'll get rid of everything, put it all away somewhere, after.'

I didn't ask her after what, because I knew: after I had found his killer. After she could find some peace.

'Do you mind if I go through his things now?'

'Ain't that why you come over here?'

A kettle whistled in the kitchen, and she went to turn it off.

'What you looking for, anyway?' she asked when she came back.

'I'll know it when I find it.'

I went through the boxes first, and there were few things with stories to tell. Tucked into an old photo album at various angles and in no order were pictures of Shawn at various ages with various women. There were about twenty CDs of contemporary female artists – Mary J., TLC, Whitney. Shawn Raymond had definitely liked the sisters. I picked up what seemed to be the most recent photo of him and studied it. He had been tall and well-built. That hint of good looks I'd seen in Rayshawn's face fulfilled in his father's. His smile was mischievous yet charming, and he had the twinkle in his eye of a man who savoured fast times and faster females; the kind who would die young and leave a roomful of pissed-off women.

One photo in a cardboard frame taken in a bar caught my attention. His arm was draped around, and he was nuzzling the neck of, a pretty young thing who had squeezed herself into him and was holding a drink in one hand and a lit cigarette in the other. She was college-girl pretty, with a short haircut, flawless brown skin, and teeth that said she'd spent her thirteenth birthday in braces. The tilt of her head, high with just a touch of arrogance, gave her a look of self-confidence and an air of entitlement, as if she deserved the best and was sure she would get it. I flipped the photo around looking for a name or a date, but there was nothing written on it. I held it up for Bessie to see. She put her hands over her eyes.

'I don't want to see his picture!'

'Can you try, Bessie? I need to know who this woman is.' She glanced at it very quickly and then looked away.

'Looks like Gina. Gina Lennox.'

There were several photos of Bessie and one of Shawn as a kid, which was bent around the edges. I didn't look too hard at the blurred images because it was one I suspected he'd taken with my brother, and I didn't feel like seeing it. I was as bad as Bessie. There was another picture of the man in the large photo in the silver frame, which was obviously a smaller copy. I picked it up and examined it.

'That's Antoine, Shawn's daddy,' Bessie volunteered before I could ask her, and I realised that it was impossible not to see the resemblance. He was handsome as his son had been. Shawn Raymond may have inherited his mother's eyes and cheekbones, but he had his father's style; it was in the carriage of his head, the gleam in his eye that could be seen despite the age of the photograph.

'This is the same man who is in the large photograph?' I nodded toward the one on the TV.

'Yeah.'

'You said he'd been shot,' I said, remembering what she'd told me in my office.

'He died about six months after that thing was taken, killed over some bullshit about nothing. Shawn ain't ever known him 'cept what he seen of him in these pictures.'

'His name was Antoine Raymond?'

'I said he was Shawn's daddy, didn't I? What's left of Shawn's clothes is in that suitcase,' she said, nodding toward the corner as if she wanted to change the subject. 'I already been through the pockets. Ain't nothing there to find. That son-of-a-bitch landlord went through his things before he sent them over here.'

The 'good stuff' Bessie had sent to Rayshawn must have been pretty damn good. What was left looked pretty good to me. There were several sweaters that felt like cashmere, three new shirts, and about a dozen Calvin Klein briefs and undershirts. There were also three pairs of black silk pyjamas. He'd obviously been a man who took stepping out the house and climbing into bed very seriously.

'He liked nice things,' I said neutrally. That Black American Princess and those black silk pyjamas would have cost him some money.

'Ain't nothing wrong with liking nice things if you can afford it.'

'And he could afford it?'

'What it look like to you?'

I folded Shawn's clothes, put them back into the suitcase, and stood back up.

'Ain't nothing there to find. I told you that,' Bessie said.

'Did Shawn ever mention somebody named Chee-chee?' I asked her.

'Chee-chee? Chee-chee what?'

'I just have that name. Chee-chee.'

'What the hell kind of name is that, Chee-chee? Is it a woman or a man?'

'I just have the name,' I repeated.

'You don't know if it's a woman or a man?' She looked at me skeptically.

'No.'

'I ain't ever heard that name, but Shawn didn't tell me his business. He was a grown man.'

'Did he spend a lot of time here? During the evening, when you were at work, maybe?'

'Why would he do that when he had his own place?'

'Could he have met somebody here in the evening when you were at work. Did he have a key?' Maybe this Chee-chee had been a night visitor he didn't want in his apartment, I thought but didn't say. Maybe he hadn't wanted her – if it was a woman – to run into his other woman, Gina Lennox. Maybe he wanted to meet Chee-chee alone. Did he want Pandora to tell him of this person's coming to warn him, or simply to let him know?

'Yeah, he had a key. He'd look in on me sometimes, make sure I was doing all right.' She lit a cigarette, inhaled, and snapped the flame of the match out so fast I thought she would sprain her wrist.

'And you leave home around six at night?'

'Six, seven.'

'And you're home in the morning around this time?'

'What you trying to get at? He wouldn't do something he wasn't supposed to do here without me giving him leave. So don't be saying nothing you ain't got no business saying!'

'I'm not saying anything that I don't have any business saying, Bessie.'

'What you trying to say then? I didn't give you all that money for you to be talking bad about my son.'

'Let's get something straight, Bessie. I took your money so I could find out who killed your son. I don't know where that will lead me or if you will like where it leads me, but that's the way this thing works. Now if you would like me to give you back your money, tell me now and I won't waste it or my time. Would you like your money back?'

'I didn't say that, did I?' she said with a pout. 'Go on and keep it.'

'The things I find out might be hard, Bessie,' I said more gently. 'You've got to decide if you really want to know what I might turn up. Sometimes it's best just to let things lay as they are, keep the good memories you have of somebody good. The truth can be very painful sometimes. It can be hard to live with.'

'Go on and find out the truth. All of it. The truth is all I have,' she said after thinking about it a moment. 'What did that man say, the truth will set you free? Well, I'm tired of being slaved by my boy's death, so that truth has got to set me free.'

But Bessie had been very defensive about the possibility that Shawn had used her apartment for something he had no business using it for. I'd gotten a sense there might be something about her son that she didn't want to admit or face. I tucked that piece of information in the back of my mind.

'I'm just trying to figure out what really happened to Shawn,' I added again.

'So when you going to start all this figuring?'

'I started as soon as you gave me your retainer.'

'So what you going to do now?'

'I'm going to talk to the Lennoxes.'

She dropped down on the couch in front of her cold uneaten breakfast. 'Will you tell them people to *please* let me see my grandbaby?' she asked in a sad, small voice.

And I did consider bringing that up as I sat in my car in front of Gus Lennox's house. But then I decided that another approach might be wiser. Despite what I'd said to Jake, I really didn't think Gus Lennox had anything to do with Shawn Raymond's murder: Jake's defense of the man's honor had counted for something. But Gina Lennox was another matter.

Instinct told me that if I was going to find out anything about Shawn Raymond and his relationship with Gina, the less I said about Bessie Raymond the better off I'd be. The trick would be to get Gus and Gina, if she was there this afternoon, to trust me enough to open up. I didn't want to gain their confidence by dropping my brother's name. Somehow it seemed disrespectful to use his memory for that purpose.

So I decided on the oldest play in the PI game book – the old I-represent-an-unclaimed-money scam, which will always loosen up somebody's lips, especially if they don't have anything to hide. I grabbed an official-looking folder, jammed some typed papers into it, spread on another layer of rum raisin lipstick, and headed toward the house.

The man opened the door so quickly I knew he'd been watching me from the window, and that threw me off balance even more than the way he looked did. He was dressed all in gray – from his faded jeans to his short-sleeved undershirt, which revealed a large, ugly scar cut so deeply into his arm it looked as if it had been carved. Even his skin had a gray pallor to it, as if all the blood had been drained out of him. His features were bloated and his receding chin was tucked into his face, giving it a flat, pushed-in look. His eyes had no life in them. *Was this Augustus Lennox?* I wondered. *Can time have done that much damage?* I studied his face carefully but could see only the slightest trace of his brother Ben in it.

'What do you want?'

He was scary, but I wasn't about to be scared. I cleared my throat, lifted my head, and met his hostility with my own. 'I'm looking for Gus Lennox. I was told this was his home,' I said, finally looking him in the face, managing to pull my eyes away from that scar.

'What you want with him?'

'I'm Tamara Hayle, Mr Lennox. Jake Richards, an attorney, gave me your address.'

'Ezekiel, who rang that bell?' Another voice, which sounded nearly identical to that of the man in front of me, rang out from another part of the house. 'Who is it, Zeke?'

The man jumped as if he was afraid, and didn't answer. Somebody bounded downstairs – two stairs at a time, it sounded like – and walked quickly across a carpeted floor. When he turned the corner and entered the short, narrow corridor to the door, I recognised him at once. The years hadn't changed him at all.

Augustus Lennox had the broad shoulders and powerful arms of a younger man and stood very straight, as if a metal pole had been rammed up his spine. Even in jeans and a wrinkled navy sweater, he had a military bearing, as if he were getting ready to salute – every inch the distinguished cop Jake had described. His hair was silver gray, and unlike the other man who stood before me, his skin was a ruddy brown, as if he'd been out in the cool autumn air raking leaves with the best of them. His smile was broad and friendly, meant to put somebody at ease. But his piercing eyes were unsettling and impossible to read. They studied me curiously.

'I know you from somewhere. And I know it's not just that you're a pretty girl first thing in the afternoon. There's something else. Damn, that face is familiar!'

'I'm Tamara Hayle. Johnny Hayle's sister,' I blurted out despite my decision not to mention it; those eyes had pulled it out of me. Johnny's name had the effect it always did. Gus looked startled for a moment, like people always do when I mention my brother and they recall how he died, but he recovered quickly, and his eyes softened.

'I haven't heard that name in fifteen years,' he said with genuine feeling. 'Come on in here, sweetheart. Zeke, why didn't you tell me Johnny Hayle's little sister was standing here at the door? I guess you met my brother Zeke?' He swept me away from Zeke and into his home.

It was a house that looked like nobody lived in it. The off-white carpet was immaculate, and the pale walls were the same creamy colour as the long leather couch that edged halfway around the room and sat across from two matching yellow armchairs. A glass coffee table gleaming like it had just been touched up with Windex displayed dainty crystal knickknacks. I could see the edge of a small baby grand piano jutting out from the door of an adjoining room. I cringed as the afternoon sun, pouring in through the sparkling windows, reminded me of what a grubby mess I'd left my own house in. From behind the swinging door that separated the dining room from the kitchen, the rosemary scent of lamb stew hit my nose, and for a fleeting moment I tried to think of a way to get myself invited to dinner – it smelled *that* good.

'My wife Mattie is a great cook,' Gus Lennox said with amusement, noticing the light that came into my eyes. 'Mattie, come in here. There's somebody you've got to meet.' A thin woman in a beige velour leisure suit came in from the kitchen and sat down next to her husband on the couch. I perched on the edge of one of the armchairs across from them, glancing behind me to see if Zeke was going to join us, but he'd disappeared.

Mattie Lennox was roughly the same age as Bessie Raymond, but the similarity stopped there. Her flawless brown skin hinted of expensive cosmetics and weekly facials. Wispy tendrils of silky iron-gray hair slipped down from the tight chignon that sat on the top of her head. Her fingernails were neatly manicured, and pearl earrings peeked subtly from her ears. Her unlined skin and straight hair pointed to a native American strain deep in her background. 'Indian blood', my grandma would have called that look. *She got some Indian blood in her.* She had the proud, poker-faced demeanour of an

71

ancient Native American woman too.

'You remember Johnny Hayle? This here is his sister, Tamara. Goddamn, if you don't look like your brother!' Gus exclaimed with obvious pleasure as he shook his head in mock disbelief. 'I loved that son of a bitch, I sure did.'

Mattie's smile was tight and forced, as if she was holding something back.'

'Would you like something to drink? Some tea?' Her voice was distant, and so soft I could barely hear her. I leaned forward, and she repeated herself.

Gus laughed heartily and shook his head. 'Too early for a drink? If you're anything like that brother of yours used to be, forget about that tea!'

'No, thank you,' I said, wanting to get his attention away from Johnny as quickly as I could.

'What brings you to this neck of the woods? You still living over there on Chestnut Terrace, or did you move to Montclair or South Orange or one of them other places folks move to when they think they're too good for Newark?'

'I'm still in East Orange. I'm a private investigator now.' A shadow passed across his eyes.

'Runs in the family. The justice thing.'

I smiled, nodded in agreement, and we chatted about nothing until I was able to ease the conversation into the reason for my visit. 'I'm afraid what brings me here isn't altogether pleasant. I'm doing some work for an insurance company. I'm afraid that it involves your family,' I said.

He shifted on the couch, and his wife stiffened. 'My family? In what way?'

I braced myself. 'A person named Shawn Raymond bought a large life insurance policy several weeks before he died, and the company is trying to find out more about his survivors before they pay his estate. He died under very sad, very mysterious circumstances. Some members of your family will be able to lay claim to the money if I'm able to answer some of the questions that need to be answered. Your daughter Gina and a child . . . Gus, I think his name was—' I hesitated for effect and took a look at the papers I'd shoved into the folder— 'were listed as survivors.' It sounded phoney because I don't like lying, so I shifted through the folder again, wishing I'd just gone on and told the man the truth.

'You came over here to ask me questions about Shawn Raymond?' Gus's voice was controlled but I could hear an undercurrent of anger, and his reddish brown skin got redder. 'That filthy son of a bitch brought his dirt into my family and now he's reaching up from his goddamn grave to touch us? I don't believe a sister of Johnny Hayle would stoop to— Listen to me, you, Tamara Hayle, any money that son of a bitch left for my daughter she don't want nothing to do with, you understand me? Any money—' He stopped suddenly as his wife put a restraining hand on his knee.

There was the rustle of silk on the stairs, and we all glanced up toward the sound. A young woman holding a baby, who looked to be about a year old, in one arm and the bannister with the other hand slowly walked downstairs.

'I heard you say his name, Daddy. Are you doing all that shouting about Shawn? Shawn is dead now, and that's what you wanted, so why don't you just let him rest in peace?'

Gus glanced up and dropped his head as if he was ashamed. 'I'm sorry, baby,' he said.

Gina Lennox squeezed between her parents on the couch and handed her baby to her mother, who kissed him on the top of his head as he snuggled into the crook of her neck.

'Don't talk about little Gus's daddy in front of him like that.

Please don't do that to him.' Gina's voice had the exact same pitch and timbre as her mother's, the same fluttery tone that made you bend forward to hear.

'I'm sorry, baby. I thought you were still asleep.' There was pain and sadness in Gus's eyes as he spoke. I felt sorry for him.

'I'm Gina,' she said, and her dark eyes focused on me. She was petite, not quite five feet tall, with a fragility about her that made her look like she'd crack if you hugged her hard. Her hair was much longer than it had been in Shawn's picture, and she wore it piled on top of her head in a loose bun like her mother's. She had on a blood-red satin robe, a gift from her dead boyfriend, I guessed. The bold colour and fabric looked as if it might be his style, not hers – certainly not now, anyway. Her voice and the hesitant, unsure way she had come downstairs all made her seem indecisive, broken, as if she were recovering from some deadly illness. The vibrancy and confidence of the girl in the photo was clearly gone.

'I'm Tamara Hayle. I'm here about an insurance claim,' I said, feeling more self-conscious about my choice of tactic with every word I uttered.

'Insurance?' Her eyes lit up.

I cleared my throat. 'Well, it's not clear yet if it will go through or how far things will go.' I spoke quickly and unconvincingly, wondering if it was too late to change my tactic without sounding like I was running a game.

'Insurance?' she asked again. 'Are you saying that Shawn left me some insurance? I knew he wouldn't forget me or little Gus. I knew that!' She stared at her father with triumph in her eyes, but Gus was studying me with his head tipped slightly to one side, the way a dog does when he listens to a sound he can't identify. I felt sick, knowing that my 'tactical' not so clever lie was setting the girl up. But it was too late to do anything but plow ahead.

'Well, it's not completely clear how the claim will pay itself out. I'm not free to divulge any more information at this early point. These things can take months, years, decades to settle, and I'm under very strict—'

'You're a fucking liar. How dare you come into this house and lie to me!' Gus Lennox said.

I was definitely caught with my drawers down, as Wyvetta Green would put it, and doubly ashamed because I knew he was speaking the truth.

'I'm sorry,' I managed to stutter out, and I was.

'Never, never, never lie to me!' His voice was hoarse, and rising from his seat, he pointed his finger at me, the small muscles in his thick neck bulging as he repeated each word. I pulled away from him, stunned by the violence in his voice and that thick finger waving so near my eye. Certain that he was going to hit me, I covered my face with my hands, my heart pounding.

And then he smiled, a smile at once sinister and triumphant. It was the smile I'd seen cops – brutal, abusive cops – smile when they watched somebody's humiliation, saw somebody weak crumble from terror and the sheer force of their presence. It was a sadist's smile that would broaden at the sight of someone's shame. I stole a quick glance at his wife and daughter. They stared straight ahead, their faces like stone.

I have always hated bullies, and that was what Gus was with his spitting words and eyes that bored into me. I hated him at that moment, with a hatred that started in the pit of my stomach and curled up through my throat. But something in me, running as deep as that hatred, would not let me be afraid. I closed my notebook with my phoney papers and shoved them to the bottom of my pocketbook. Then I looked him in the eye.

'I told you I was sorry, and there's nothing more I'm going to say. I couldn't think of any other way to get you to share the facts with me,' I said, my voice even.

'Who the fuck sent you over here?'

'I represent a client, who wants his name kept confidential.'

'You think I'm stupid! The minute you told me what you did for a living, the minute that dead bastard's name came out of your mouth, I knew what you were up to. Get the fuck out of here!'

I picked up my things, ready to do what he said.

But then Gina spoke in her soft, scared voice. 'Please wait a minute. I don't care why she is here, Daddy. I don't care who sent her or if she lied to us. If it's about Shawn, I want to talk to her.' Her fear told me that she didn't often defy him, and that she would pay a price for it, but she didn't care. I focused my attention on her now, glad not to have to look at Gus.

'Thank you, Gina. I'd like you to answer a few questions for me. I'm sorry I wasn't more forthright—'

'It doesn't matter.' Her eyes filled with tears.

'Shut up, Gina,' Gus said.

'Daddy—'

'The question is, who hired you. One of his tramps, his junkie whore mama, his—'

'Please don't do this, Daddy!'

'I'm sorry, baby. The cops went through this with us already. Go talk to them,' he said to me, his eyes narrowing in anger.

'If you don't mind, I'd just like to know anything you can tell me about him, about people he knew, why your father hated him so much.' I addressed her again, tacking that on.

'I didn't hate him. I hated what he did to my daughter, what he made her become,' he answered for her, his voice more reasonable. 'And she knew it soon enough too, didn't you, Gina? Even though you know how much I love this little guy, little Gus here. We all knew that he just wasn't right for you. Didn't you finally understand that, baby? Didn't you?'

'What did he make her become?'

Gina dropped her head, and the question stayed unanswered.

I asked another, ignoring the glaring eyes of Gus. 'Had you seen him near the time of his death?'

'She had left him by then,' Gus answered for her.

'Is that right, Gina?'

'Yes. He's right,' she said, not looking at him.

'She knew by then that he wasn't shit, didn't you by then, baby?'

'Yes.'

'And there was no way in hell she was going to bring that filth back into our lives, were you, baby?'

'Stop it,' Gina said.

'Mrs Lennox?'

'My husband speaks for both of us. He speaks for our family.' Mattie spoke with a steely defiance that surprised me.

'I'm sorry,' Gus said to Gina and then to me. 'I'm sorry, Tamara. I'm sorry.' He dropped his head into his hands. The abrupt change in his manner was stunning.

What the hell was he up to?

'This whole last couple of months. Since that man's death, his murder, how it happened, my daughter's grief, my lack of it, has taken its toll on my family. I'll help you now, if that's what my baby wants.' He reached over and took his daughter's hand.

'Where were you on April twenty-fifty?' I got to the point quickly. I didn't know what game he was playing, and I wanted to score some points before he quit.

77

'We answered this for the police.'

'Would you answer it for me?'

The cat smile of triumph came to his lips again. 'Where were we, Mattie? Had we left Costa Rica by then?' He leaned back against the couch.

'Costa Rica?' I put my pencil down.

'As in Puerto Caldero. I almost missed that damn boat – if that kid hadn't seen me coming to make it to the last launch, I don't know what I would have done.' He chuckled and nodded, and his wife chuckled with him.

'I kept telling you the ship was leaving,' she said, as coy as a kitten.

'Hold it. You were all out of the country?'

'Yeah, Costa Rica.' Gus turned back to me, with nothing in his eyes. 'My wife, me, and my brother Ben and his wife – ex-wife now I guess, they just separated – were on a cruise together, the good ship *Odyssey* for ten days, Panama Canal cruise. We got one of those good deals. Ben – you remember Ben – and his wife Vera came along for half-price.'

'You're telling me you were on a cruise during that time?' I interrupted him, still not getting it.

'Yeah, that's what I'm telling you. You hard of hearing, Tamara Hayle?'

Bastard, I said to myself.

He continued. 'Me, my wife, Mattie, my brother Ben, and his wife, Vera, were on one of those ten-day cruises in the lower Caribbean. We left the Sunday before the twenty-fifth – when was it, Mattie? The twenty-first? Was it Cartagena on the twenty-fifth or the stop before in Costa Rica, where we got that coffee that Ben liked so much, that Tres Dias, or something?'

'Tres Ríos. It was Costa Rica,' Mattie said, her eyes never leaving mine.

'If you want to see our passports, talk to our travel agent, the captain of the ship. Sweetheart, I told all this to the cops, and they checked out everything, from the stamps on each of our passports verifying when we entered and left the country, to the day and time we came back in. The State Department is serious about these things these days, seeing we got all these illegals trying to get into our country nowadays. We were on a cruise off the coast of Colombia when that piece of filth was murdered, so if that was what you came here to bother us with, you wasted your goddamn time.'

'And you?' I asked Gina.

'Gina and her sister Lena were at a party,' Gus answered for her. 'They were over there in South Orange, didn't get in until two. They were both there, their friends can vouch for that. The baby was here with a sitter.'

'And Zeke?'

Gus was suddenly angry and exasperated again. 'Look, we told everything to the cops, they checked everything out. Have you talked to the officer who worked this case yet? Didn't believe what he told you, huh?' Sheepishly, I was forced to admit that I hadn't talked to the police about it.

His smile was smug. 'So you think you got it over the cops? I thought you said you were a licensed investigator. That's one of the first things you do, little sister, investigate what's been investigated before.'

'I haven't been anybody's little sister in more than fifteen years, Gus. You can drop that shit right now,' I said.

'Do you think one of us had something to do with this?' He spat the words out. 'Here.' He snatched my notebook off the table and scribbled a name and telephone number across one of the pages. 'Call him.'

I snatched it back without looking at it. 'I'm just trying to find out what happened to the man.'

'Let me give you some advice, one old cop to somebody who should know better. You're barking up the wrong tree. Check on some of his friends, his women friends. The low-life people he knew. I couldn't stand him. I made no secret of that. He had no right coming anywhere near my daughter. He shouldn't even be on the same planet as my family, but goddamn if I'd be stupid enough to kill the son of a bitch.'

'Do any of you know somebody called Chee-chee?'

Mattie Lennox stiffened so slightly I wouldn't have noticed it if I hadn't been looking for it.

'No,' Gus said flatly.

'Do you, Mrs Lennox? Gina?' I asked, knowing damn well I wouldn't get anything from them.

'No,' they said in unison.

'Gina, would it be possible for me to talk to you alone at some point?' I asked quickly, and she glanced at her father before she answered me, more loudly than she needed to.

'Yes,' she said, and scribbled a telephone number down on my notepad.

'I'll give you a call very shortly, okay?'

'Yes.' She avoided everyone's eyes as she spoke.

The three of us sat there for half a minute, the room silent except for the baby's snores. The smell of something burning floated in from the kitchen, giving everybody the excuse they needed to leave. Mattie, with a furtive glance at her husband, handed the baby back to her daughter and rushed toward the smell. Gina, hoisting her dozing child to her shoulder, headed back upstairs. I stood, pulled out my business card and gave it to Gus, who studied it like he'd never seen one before.

'Thank you for your time,' I said, trying to mask my anger with professional detachment.

'Hey listen, Tamara. I hope I wasn't too hard on you?' He said it like he meant it.

'Hard on me? For what, Gus? Jumping all over me? No, Gus. You weren't too hard. Just a mean, ill-tempered son of a bitch.' He'd given me the in, and I couldn't resist saying it.

He laughed a good-natured chuckle. 'You sound like your brother.'

Go fuck yourself, I thought but didn't say.

'Look, I'm sorry. I been losing it a lot. This whole thing has been bad for me. The goddamn cops put us through hell, put me through hell, despite who I am, probably *because* of who I am. It was their chance, the bastards, to fuck with me and my family, and they pulled out everything they could get on me. Everybody knew how I felt about that bastard, but I didn't have anything to do with his death, and everybody knows it now.' He cast his eyes down. 'I was real close to your brother, Tamara.'

I wiped everything out of my eyes and off my face.

'I'm short with people sometimes. Nasty, like I was with you just now. I know I didn't have any right to be cursing at you like that.' He kept his eyes dropped as if he was embarrassed. 'It comes from being a cop for so long. I wouldn't want you to think bad of me or my family because of my rude attitude. I wouldn't want you to hold it against me. I don't use language like that around ladies. I don't know what came over me. Will you forgive a rude old man with a filthy mouth?'

I studied him, wondering what his game was.

'I'm sorry, Tamara. But the very thought of that man still tears me up, may his soul rest in peace. I didn't kill him. I think my daughter thinks I did, sometimes, but I didn't. I couldn't have. I wish they'd find the bastard who did it so my daughter would quit blaming me. My daughter is the only thing

81

in my life that is important to me. The only thing.'

What about the other one?

'There are no hard feelings,' I finally said.

He smiled that welcoming grin that had greeted me when I saw him. 'You used to go out with my brother Ben, didn't you?' he asked offhandedly as he walked me to the door.

'We went out to dinner a couple of years ago.' Avoiding his eyes, I shifted things around in my bag again like I was looking for my keys.

'Have you heard from him recently?'

'No, I haven't.'

'He's still in Connecticut, but he's been thinking of settling down around here. Would you mind if I gave him your card? He's been pretty down for the last couple of months. His marriage broke up right after we got back from our vacation. It would be good for him to take out a pretty woman. Cheer him up. If it's okay. It wouldn't be a conflict of interest, would it?' I decided to let that touch of sarcasm in his voice pass.

'Sure,' I said. 'It would be nice to hear from him.'

But I wondered what in the hell he was up to, tossing his baby brother at me like that.

'Thank you again for your time,' I added, with a smile that could melt coal.

'It was my pleasure.'

'I'll bet it was, you bastard,' I muttered to myself as I walked to my car.

I don't know where it comes from, that intuitive sense of danger I get when something bad is about to cross my path. I think from my long-dead grandma who raised me more than my mother did. I got it as I glanced back for one last look at the Lennox house and caught a glimpse of something in the window, someone all in gray, hunched close and staring like a cat does before it springs.

This is a house of evil secrets, I thought, and a chill went through me.

Six

'You ain't no cop,' Rayshawn Rudell said. I tensed at the sound of his voice. He had a sour smell about him, like he hadn't washed or changed his clothes in a couple of days.

'I know your grandma, boy. Watch yourself.'

'Why you tell me you were a cop?' I was walking the same route I'd walked that night but from the parking lot this time, and it was morning instead of night, two weeks to the day since his grandmother had stepped into my office. He walked fast to keep up, glancing around him like he was expecting somebody to join us.

'You're just about the last person I expected to see this morning, Rayshawn. Forget your gat?'

'How you know my name?'

'I told you. I know your grandmother.'

'Did you tell her?' His voice sounded anxious, or maybe I was just imagining it. But he did seem younger than before, all skinny arms, ashy skin, and eyes that might haunt some woman till the end of her days – if he lived long enough. But he looked and smelled like he was coming apart.

'That's the last thing your grandmother needs to know about you. What made you pull that stupid stunt the other night? Don't you know how dumb that was?'

'I needed myself some money.' He glanced up nervously and

85

then dropped his eyes. I wondered if he was high on something.

'That could have landed your little butt right in jail.'

'What you going to do about it? You ain't no cop.'

'No, but I know enough cops to put your behind away. And don't think just because I'm standing here talking to you like you've got some sense that I've forgotten what happened.' I slowed my pace, and he caught up. 'Where did you get that .38? Guns aren't cheap.'

'It wasn't no Glock or nothing like that.'

'How long have you had it?'

'Long enough to do what I need to do with it.' He threw me a wolfish grin.

We walked a minute or two without saying anything. I wondered what he was doing back here, and then recalled that Bessie said his foster parents lived nearby. 'You visiting somebody?' I asked him, but he ignored the question.

'You knew my daddy?'

I turned to face him, trying to read what was in those eyes. 'I knew him once.'

He changed directions. 'Don't go nowhere near my mama, you hear me? I don't care what my grandma say. And I know you ain't no cop now.' He tried to add the menace of the other night, but it didn't work.

'You don't know anything about me, son.'

'I ain't your goddamn son.' He turned and walked away, at a leisurely pace this time, like he didn't give a damn, but I noticed that his gait was slow and unsteady.

When I got to my office I booted up my computer and pulled up the file YBGB, looking for the name of Rayshawn's foster parents, which I remembered as being Layton and who were listed in the phone book. I also checked my notebook for the name of the detective that Gus Lennox had given me. I could barely make out the G-something Osborne he'd scribbled down, but the phone number was clear.

Before I dialled it I called my old boss, Captain Roscoe L. DeLorca of the Belvington Heights Police Department, and told him I was working on a case and needed to verify somebody's alibi. I asked if he'd call the cop in charge and put in a good word for me so I wouldn't have to go in cold. Although he would never acknowledge it, DeLorca feels he owes me for the racist, sexist shit his men piled on me before I left his force. In his burly, tobacco-smelling way, he'd tried to be a mentor of sorts to me, and he still has my back covered when I need it. He's one of the few white men I trust completely, and I'd bet serious money that I'm the only black woman with whom he has ever had more than a passing word. We're friends, uneasily connected in ways that people who know us both find puzzling, but I knew he would do this favour for me.

After I finished with DeLorca, I called the number Gus Lennox had given me, telling G-something Osborne's answering machine where I'd gotten his name and asking if he could verify some information. That done, I scrolled to the top of the file on my screen, studied the names typed across it, and wondered aloud why each and every one of them would want Shawn Raymond dead.

Nothing came to me, so I left my office and walked down the hall to fill my kettle with water from the sink in the bathroom, then gazed out my window at nothing in particular while I waited for it to boil. Then I made a cup of chamomile tea, hoping it would ease my brain into action. I typed in 'Rayshawn Rudell' and the word 'SON' in capital letters, hoping for some kind of inspiration. He was son to both Viola Rudell, whose name he carried, and Shawn Raymond, whose name he didn't.

Was it possible that he could have killed his father?

I thought about that crazy mix of hormones, wildness, and just plain foolishness that make up the soul of teenage boys.

Just what are our intentions, honorable or otherwise, toward my mother? Jamal's crack to Jake – his protective stance and unusual suspicion – had stunned me. The older he got the less sure I was of what would come out of his mouth. I thought I knew him, but growing into manhood was something I was obviously not equipped to fully understand. Jamal had some serious anger toward his father, my ex-husband DeWayne Curtis, too, and it popped out these days more often than it used to in strange ways and with startling intensity.

How deep could an angry son's rage go?

Jamal had me and a crew of other folks to correct him when he needed correcting. All Rayshawn had was a former crack addict for a grandma and a mother who had cut up a young girl's face, a woman more capable of using her son's anger for her own dark purposes.

Don't go nowhere near my mama.

'VIOLA RUDELL.' I wrote her name down in capital letters and the name Chee-chee underneath it.

'GUS LENNOX.' I jotted down my thoughts about him in random, free-form notes: 'Good guy/good cop; honor and tradition; tough; mean; kind? grilled by his own; respected by his own; hated by his own?' I also put down a note to call the cruise line that he and his wife had sailed on, though I was sure he wouldn't lie about something that could be so easily checked.

'ZEKE LENNOX.' Now that was one evil son of a bitch. What was his story and where had he been that night?

'MATTIE LENNOX.' Sister liked herself a clean house, that was for damn sure. No dust balls or greasy fingerprints there.

Some mothers liked to live their fantasies through their daughters, but Shawn Raymond had been an honest-to-God mother's nightmare. Or had he? I only had Gus Lennox's word on that.

'LENA LENNOX.' The silent twin Gus Lennox had forgotten when he started carrying on about fatherly love.

'GINA LENNOX.' I had called Gina three times trying to set up an appointment so we could talk alone, and she had never bothered to call me back, which told me she was probably not interested in doing it. Maybe Gus had gotten to her. But the truth was, even though she had agreed to talk, there was no legal reason for her to do it if she didn't want to. I ain't no cop, as Rayshawn had pointed out. But she was bound to have some useful information about Lena and the girlfriend they had both been with that night. Could there have been more drama to come in her relationship with Shawn, another shoe to drop? Which brought me back to Shawn Raymond, who he was and why he had died like he had. I called the Lennox number again, and left another message for Gina to call me, fearing now that she probably wouldn't – for whatever reasons.

Don't go nowhere near my mama.

Why?

When the phone rang I jumped, then answered it with professional abruptness, hoping it was Gina, assuming it was the cop.

But it was neither.

'I can't tell you how glad I was to get your card from my brother,' said Ben Lennox in his low baritone. I sat up straight, saving the screen with the names of his family members on it and logging out of my computer in one quick, guilty motion.

'Ben?' I asked, knowing damn well who it was.

His earthy, sexy laugh told me he was no longer that shy kid

who'd held my hand when we were teenagers or even the other
who'd held the rest of me when we made love that one night
long ago.

'In the flesh.' I smiled despite myself. 'How have you been,
Tamara Hayle?'

'I've been fine. And how about you? How have you been?
What a surprise to hear from you,' I lied, probably not
convincingly.

'I've seen better days.'

There was an awkward silence, and we both spoke at once
to fill it. He stopped, still the gentleman, permitting me to
continue.

'So, are you still living in Connecticut?' Gus had mentioned
he was thinking about moving, but I didn't know if he'd done
it yet.

He paused for half a second. 'Yes. My firm transferred me to
the main branch, from the one in New Haven to Manhattan.
How about you? Gus mentioned that you're in law enforcement.'

'I guess you could call it that. I own a private investigation
firm.' I didn't mention it was a firm of one. I also wondered if
he was playing the same game as me, not telling all he knew.
'I'm about the same – older, poorer, plumper.'

'Isn't everybody? Still living in the same place?'

'My parents' place. Except for my sister, I'm the only one
left standing. I mean—' I grimaced at how tasteless the crack
came out sounding and searched for words.

'I know what you mean,' he cut me off gently. 'You don't
have to explain to me. So things are basically going okay?'

'Basically.'

'How's your son? Is it Jamal? He must be a teenager by
now. Damn, time goes fast, doesn't it?'

'Too fast.'

There was another silence, but not as uncomfortable, and I heard him sigh on the other end. 'That's the one thing I regret, about my marriage ending like it did.'

'I was sorry to hear that, Ben, about your marriage.'

'Not as much as me. I really miss her, my wife. I loved her. But what I miss more is the loss of my dreams, our dreams. Having kids was definitely one of them. We tried for a long time. We were still trying when it ended,' he added with surprising candour.

'You've still got time, Ben. The rest of your life. That biological clock doesn't run out for men.'

'Yeah, but the older you get the tougher it is to find a woman who you want to have kids with, believe me. I was sure I'd found her.'

'If it's anything like finding a good man, I believe you.' We both laughed at that, two divorced people sharing hard times; for a moment anyway, we had something in common. 'But you haven't been looking very long, have you?' I wondered when he was going to get to why he'd called me.

Why his brother had asked him to call me?

'I don't have time for the dating game anymore. I'm just too tired – that who-is-going-to-call-each-other-first stuff and the rest of it is for kids.'

'But men make all the rules, Ben. You do the asking. And the choosing.' I immediately regretted the shrill rise of my voice.

'There's a lot of chaff to go through until you get the wheat. Most of the time, I just don't have the energy to sift.'

'There are a lot of good women out there, Ben,' I said, telling what I knew was the truth, not feeling sorry for him.

'Which, Tamara Hayle, brings me to the reason for my call.' He eased into it with a chuckle that made me smile.

'And what is that, Ben?'

91

'Come on, Tamara, we've known each other too long to be coy.'

'Not very long. And not for a while.'

'Will you go out with me tonight?' he asked bluntly.

'I don't think so, Ben.'

'Is it that tonight it a bad night, or that every night will be a bad night?'

'The latter.'

'Hmm.'

'Sorry.'

'If you don't want to go out with someone with the last name of Lennox, I more than understand. I hear my older brother made a real fool of himself the other day. What can I say? He's a jackass sometimes. But he has nothing to do with this,' he added too quickly.

'Nothing, Ben?'

'I haven't taken his advice about who to date since I asked you to the prom that time.'

We both laughed at that, comfortably, like we *had* known each other for a long time. 'I don't hold your brother against you. But I have some reservations about going out with you . . . for obvious reasons.'

'Not so obvious to me.'

'Did your brother tell you what I'm working on?'

'A little.'

'Then you know it involves your family.'

His pause made me wish I could see his face. 'Do you really think Gus or maybe my niece had something to do with Shawn Raymond's death?'

'I don't know.'

'I can tell you honestly that none of us had anything to do with it.'

'I wish I could say that's enough, but it's not,' I said, playing it real.

'No. I guess you can't.'

'I'm sorry, Ben.'

'I understand. No, I really do. But if you change your mind, I'd love to take you out. Maybe after this whole thing is over. Will you think about it?'

I paused. 'Sure, I'll think about it.'

There was that awkward silence again. Ben broke it. 'Always said what was on your mind, didn't you? No games with you, Tamara Hayle. I always respected that about you.'

'Always? Ben, we haven't spoken to each other in years. You really haven't known me since we were kids.'

'Not kids, Tamara. Young, but not kids. Not the last time.'

'It was good talking to you, Ben.' The mention of that second time around made me uncomfortable, and I was eager to get off the line.

'If you change your mind?'

'I won't.'

'Then, take good care of yourself, Tamara Hayle.'

'I always do, Ben,' I said, and hung up.

The minute I put the phone down it rang again. Despite what I'd just said, I was flattered that he was trying again so quickly and I smiled as I answered it. 'Ben?' I asked, my voice flirtatious.

'Naw, it ain't Ben. Is this Tamara Hayle, of the Tamara Hayle Investigative Services?' said G-something Osborne, gruff and efficient.

'This is Tamara Hayle,' I said, gruff and efficient right back. I quickly reviewed with him what I'd said in my message, emphasizing I'd gotten his number and name from Gus Lennox and was calling at his suggestion.

'Who did you say you were working for?'

'I didn't.' He might be as hostile to the mention of Bessie Raymond's name as Gus Lennox had been at the mention of Shawn's, even though as a cop, he was supposed to be working for her.

'You said Gus Lennox asked you to call me?' His voice implied that he didn't believe me and planned to verify it, which told me something right there. 'I'm not giving you nothing unless I know where the information might go.'

'I'm working for the deceased's mother,' I admitted.

There was a pause. 'You mean he had one?'

'We all have mothers, Detective Osborne, and this one is grieving the same way mine or yours would – if you have one,' I couldn't resist adding, not disguising my irritation.

'That case is pretty much closed.'

'Then you found out who killed Shawn Raymond?'

'I didn't say that.'

'Then it's not closed, right?' *Niggers killing niggers?*

'How can I help you, Mizz Hayle?'

'Shawn Raymond was shot on April twenty-fifth, around midnight, right?'

'Right.'

'Do you know what calibre bullet?'

He paused for about a minute, as if deciding what to tell me. He finally said, 'They pulled a .38 slug out of his heart. Right out of his heart,' he repeated with what sounded like admiration. I paused a moment before I wrote down what he'd said and underlined it.

'You're sure it was a .38?' *Could an angry son's rage go that deep?*

'Isn't that what I said? Where is this going, and how did you say you spell your name?' he asked, letting me know he

94

was taking down his own set of notes. I wondered if DeLorca had called him and then realized that Osborne wouldn't have bothered to call me at all if he hadn't.

'H-a-y-l-e. My brother Johnny used to work in your department. A very long time ago.' Cops remember their own even if only by reputation, and to the end, Johnny had had the respect of everybody who had ever heard of him, even if they hated what he'd done to himself.

'So Lennox told you to call me?'

'Yes, he did.'

'And what else do you want to know – off the record.'

'Do you know anything else about the gun?'

'No.'

'I'm not a reporter, Detective Osborne, and anything you tell me will go no farther than—'

'That's all you're getting,' he interrupted me, and I changed directions.

'Did the alibis offered by the Lennox family members on the time and date of Shawn Raymond's murder all check out?'

'If they didn't we would have brought them in. It happened last April.'

'Everything checked out completely?'

'Completely.'

'You talked to the cruise line and checked out their passports?'

'Didn't I just say to you that it all checked out?' he said with genuine irritation.

'And they all returned home, back to the States after Shawn Raymond's body was found?'

'Yeah, a couple of days after.'

'Except for the daughters?'

'The daughters had sound alibis.'

95

'And the other brother?'

He paused. 'Yeah, him too. The best you can have.' He added what sounded like a chuckle.

'And what is that?'

'Just what I said,' he snapped, in a tone that told me I wouldn't get anything more. I knew I'd have to ask somebody else.

'The girls are twins, right? Do you think that may have put a twist into things?'

'A twist? What are you talking about? Listen, I said it all checked out and it all checked out.'

'So where are you now with it?'

'What do you mean where am I now?'

'Just what I said. The statute of limitations doesn't run out on murder, does it?'

'We're still looking. If you find out anything, let me know,' he said sarcastically.

'Do you mind, sir, if I ask you one more question?' I asked sweetly, adding that 'sir' business in an attempt to soften him up. It didn't do any good.

'What?' he barked.

'Why were you so rough on Gus Lennox?'

'Rough? What do you mean?'

'Quote, "The goddamn cops put us through hell, put me through hell, despite who I am, because of who I am. It was their chance, the bastards, to fuck with me and my family, and they pulled out everything they could get on me." Unquote.'

'That's what Gus said?'

'Yep.'

He chuckled.

'So you – his former colleagues – were pretty rough on him, huh?'

He chuckled again. 'A grilling is what a grilling does, right, Mizz Tamara Hayle? Are we finished with this? I got work to do.'

'Yes, we are. Thank you very much, Detective Osborne, for your time.'

'Tell DeLorca to kiss my ass next time you see him, okay?' He hung up, and I sat there mulling over what he'd just said, glanced again at my note of Layton, the name of Rayshawn's foster parents, then dialed Ben Lennox's number to tell him I'd changed my mind.

I met him that night in a restaurant I go to only if somebody else is paying. The Pinnacle was perched high on a hill in one of those suburbs where the white folks ran when they ran out of Newark. The large pale yellow room was mostly windows, trimmed in mahogany and lit by what seemed a thousand tiny candles. It was all very discreet and elegant – a place designed for people who were going places or had been there. I'd come in late, and Ben Lennox stood and pulled out my chair like the gentleman somebody raised him to be. I liked that. Some of the guys I'd been out with in the last few years would have raced me for it.

'Well, the years have definitely been sweet to you,' Ben said after we'd ordered our drinks and settled down. I could have said the same thing about him. Ben Lennox had definitely fulfilled that promise he'd had as a kid. He was still good-looking – easy on the eyes, my grandma would have put it. Clear, chestnut-coloured skin, deep brown eyes, neatly trimmed moustache topping lips that grinned just a bit too quickly. He'd added some serious muscle over the years, but his hands when he took mine between them were gentle, and his nails were manicured and buffed – as well cared for as his suit, which was navy and expensive and accented by a striped silk tie, French-cuffed shirt, and subtle silver cuff links. The whole package was topped off by a lingering whisper of Herrera for Men cologne. A solid, respectable kind of brother, the type you could trust with your heart or your money. Wyvetta Green would have approved.

We sipped our drinks for a while – ladylike chardonnay for me, macho-man bourbon and water for him – and then, at my urging, he began filling in his life for me: what he'd done in the years since I'd known him, the kind of jobs he had, his hopes for his future, what he liked to do in his spare time. I listened and cooed and listened and cooed – the quintessential perfect date, hanging on to every word, chuckling every now and again, sharing next to nothing about my own life and dreams. But there was method to this madness. I wanted to give him the space to give me the dirt on his family.

G-something Osborne's chuckle – that know-it-all, smart-ass little grunt of a laugh – had told me Gus Lennox was still part of the tribe, and that that 'grilling' he'd supposedly gotten had probably been about as rough as a good-ol'-boy wink and a brotherly pat on the butt. Grilling was what grilling had done, which had been damn well nothing in this case and he knew it. Posing as an interested, disorganized tourist, I'd called the Odyssey Adventures cruise line before I left my office and questioned the exasperated representative about the dates, arrivals, and departures of the cruise ship *Odyssey* in April, and everything Gus had told me held up. But it all seemed too cute, and I sensed that something else was up. I just wasn't sure what.

They had pulled a .38 slug 'right out his heart,' as Osborne had put it, and I wasn't sure what that meant. One shot, one kill. It could have been luck – somebody shooting a man straight through the heart like that. The gun could have been held by a novice, like a kid who wasn't very tall and was scared and just held the gun and shot straight out in front of him with his eyes closed. Or it could have been held by an expert, who knew just how to stand and just where to aim so the bullet met its mark. There was simply no way to tell.

Rayshawn Rudell did own a .38, I knew that for a fact. But there are a lot of .38s in this world. Despite the nasty side of him I'd seen, I couldn't forget that he was still a kid, about the same age as my son, and I didn't want to think about an anger that could run deep enough to turn him into a patricidal killer. I knew I needed to find out more about Rayshawn and his mother, but I also needed more on the Lennoxes. Gus had lied about that grilling he'd gotten from Osborne, and where there's a lie there's always a reason for it. Ben Lennox was the best source I had going on Gus Lennox and his family. I also had to admit that I was curious about Ben Lennox himself too – after all these years.

'I've been doing all the talking ever since we sat down. Are you as sick of hearing my voice as I am?' Ben joked after about fifteen minutes of a nonstop monologue.

'Oh, no. I'm just enjoying listening.' I smiled demurely and took a sip of wine.

'Tell me about yourself.'

'Not much to tell.'

'Why don't you start off with what made you change your mind about tonight, all of a sudden, like you did.' There was a hint of suspicion in his voice, so I answered with the truth.

'Curiosity.'

'Curiosity?' He looked at me with doubtful eyes but a smile played on his lips.

'Yes. Weren't you curious?'

'Initially, yes. That's why I called.'

'So it wasn't just because your brother told you to do it?' I threw my first jab. Very light. Very playful. He took a quick swallow of his drink and dodged it.

'Want something to eat?'

'Calamari looks good,' I said with a glance at the menu, and Ben signalled the waitress, a blonde dressed in black who grinned too much.

'You want the truth, I guess,' he said after he'd ordered.

'Do you have something to hide?'

'I didn't say that.'

'So why did Gus want you to call me?'

'I don't know if he really did. My brother works in mysterious ways.'

'What does that mean?'

'He just told me you looked good, which you do, and that it might do me some good to look up an old girlfriend, which it has.'

'Girlfriend?'

'His word, not mine.'

'What did he say exactly?'

'You really want to know all this?' He looked a bit uncomfortable, but I pushed on anyway.

'Yeah, I do, if you don't mind.'

'No, I don't mind. Well . . .' He paused for a moment as if trying to recall the words. 'He said, "Johnny Hayle's baby sister came over here about some stupid shit that don't make no sense, but she's a fox so why don't you give her a call, might make you feel better?"' He smiled and nodded. 'That's about it.'

I didn't smile back. 'And he didn't ask you to find out what I was up to? To use your masculine charms to see if I had something on him I shouldn't have?'

'My God, woman, give yourself some credit. And if he did, do you really think I would tell you?' he added with a mischievous edge.

'Of course not.'

'But he didn't. He just handed me your card, and I realized it was a good idea so I called.'

'And this has nothing to do with Shawn Raymond?'

'I'm not saying that either.'

'At least you're being honest.' I took a sip of my drink, wondering if that was what he was being.

'Listen, Tamara, *this* is the truth. It doesn't have anything to do with Shawn Raymond as far as *I'm* concerned. I never even met the dude, never even saw him, so I have never had beef – as the kids like to say – with the brother. But to be honest, I can't speak for Gus, or what he expects of me or you or what his motives were for suggesting we go out.' With a mock look of suspicion, he glanced around his back, to his side, and under the table. 'But do you see him crawling around here anywhere? This is *our* date, right? Not our date with Augustus Lennox.'

I smiled in spite of myself.

'My brother is my brother. I know he's a pain in the butt a lot of the time, always has been. I know he's a control freak, always been that too, which is one reason I moved as far away from Jersey as I could. But Gus doesn't control my life. He'd probably like to, like he does everybody else's, but he never will.' He picked up my hand and held it for a moment, and then let it go.

I rocked back slightly in my chair, studying him.

'Now, I want some truth from you,' he said.

'From me?'

'Play fair, Tamara.'

'Okay.'

'You came out tonight because you wanted to use your *feminine* charms to find out something on my family, right?'

'Not entirely.'

'At least *you're* honest.'

'So then we both have ulterior motives?'

'I don't,' he said, like he meant it. 'I don't have time for games either, Tamara, like I said on the phone. I'm just too damned tired of them.' He looked annoyed for a minute, as if he might get up and leave, and then spoke again. 'Vera just left me – indirectly because of my family, I might add, but she had too much class to admit it and I never pushed it. My wife could never really understand the strength of the bond I have with my brothers. For better and worse.

'You're married for a couple of years and all the women you might want to take out are involved with somebody else or so mad at you for not calling them back and not being the man you probably should have been that most of them won't give you the time of day.' I glanced up surprised, wondering if he realized he was talking about what had passed between us, but he continued talking, not even aware that he had touched on the small bone I had to pick with him.

'I always liked you, even when I was a kid, so when I heard your name I gave you a call. As simple as that. If you want to forget it, I'll understand and we can go out again after this whole thing is through,' he added as he took a long swallow of his drink and gave me a charming smile. 'Hey listen, I don't mind waiting for a good thing.'

'How do you know I'm such a good thing?'

'You don't walk the roads I've walked and not know a good thing when it crosses your path.'

'I never date people who are even remotely related to a case

102

I'm working on,' I said seriously.

'In a town like this I guess you don't go out much, huh?' he said lightly, teasing me.

'Well,' I drawled, and we both laughed because I'd started to think maybe I was wrong about everything after all. It certainly wouldn't be the first time. 'I guess one drink won't hurt. But I'm warning you now – anything, I mean anything, you say may be used against you.' I was only half kidding.

'I consider myself warned,' he said, holding up his drink in a toast.

'But can you say that for the rest of your family?' I *had* warned him.

'I can only speak for myself. I'm trying very hard to cut the strings with the rest of my family, my big brother anyway.'

'Then why are you thinking about moving back to Jersey?'

'Who told you that?'

'Gus.'

'When hell freezes over.'

I left that alone as I sampled the fried calamari which had just been placed before us. They were crisp yet tender and the sauce that accompanied them had just enough tang and spice to make them interesting. Ben brooded over his drink as I gobbled them up.

'Goddamn that man!' he said out of nowhere.

I dabbed some sauce off my lips with a napkin and glanced up at him. 'Where did that come from?'

'Don't even ask.'

'Can I ask you something?' He nodded as he took one of the remaining calamari.

'What did you mean when you said your wife left you because of your family?'

'Indirectly, because of my family.'

103

'Didn't she meet them before you got married?'

Ben beckoned for the waitress to bring another order, and I, realizing that I'd cleaned up the plate nearly by myself, was embarrassed for a minute – but just for a minute.

'You know my brother, right?' He settled back, still nursing his drink. 'I mean, you've seen him in action.'

'No, not really.'

'But you know how he is. Don't try to be polite, Tamara. Mattie told me how he lit into you about Shawn Raymond. You know how he is.'

I nodded that I did.

'Gus takes over a room. He'll take over your life if you let him. He sucks up all the air so nobody else can breathe. He's always been that way, even when I was a kid.'

'Well, I can see—'

'You can't see nothing, baby. Gus—' He sighed. 'Hell.' He shook his head in exasperation, and I saw the light in his eyes turn dark.

'What's wrong, Ben?'

'Maybe we should change the subject.'

'Maybe we should,' I said, wondering if perhaps I wasn't playing as fair with him as he might be playing with me. But on the other hand, I *had* warned him.

'I don't think I can. You can never leave home, can you?' he said after a few moments.

I waxed philosophical. 'The truth of it is, home never leaves you.'

'I hated him for a long time when I was younger, and then later for the way he treated Mattie and the girls. I've seen him be brutal, abusive, and I hated the fear I used to see in their faces, even though he would never physically hurt them, never, and it's certainly not as bad as it used to be. He has always

104

been a very strict taskmaster with those girls. He didn't give them any room to grow or make mistakes. I love my brother but sometimes I can't stand him. Love him, don't like him.'

I remembered how I'd felt about Gus Lennox's bullying the day I met him, and nodded that I knew what he meant. My understanding went deeper than Gus Lennox. I'd had that kind of relationship with my mother, the love and yearning for her approval coupled with the disgust and anger at her cruelty. Yes, I understood how Ben felt about his brother in ways I wasn't yet ready to share with him.

'I look at my brothers—' he said, bringing me back to our conversation.

'Gus?'

'And Zeke. My oldest brother. You've seen him. How does he strike you?'

I searched for diplomatic words, but Ben supplied them.

'Dead. He seems dead.'

'That's not the word I was looking for.'

'It's what describes him, though, isn't it?'

Like the life was sucked out of him. 'Then Zeke is older than Gus?'

'Yeah, by about five years. But Gus dominates him the way he does everybody else. My brother sends that theory about middle children – that they're the peacemakers of the family – right down the toilet.'

'What happened to him?'

'Zeke? Drugs. Alcohol. Name it – if it could hurt him he dropped it, drank it, shot it, or smoked it. Zeke has been in trouble since he was a kid,' he added grimly.

'He's still doing them?'

'He's been in and out of jail for years. He's a haunted, damaged man, and Gus feels responsible for him in ways that

I still don't understand, which is why he lives with them. He literally has nowhere else to go.'

'It was good of Gus to take him in,' I said. 'Was he there when you all were on the cruise?'

'Zeke was in jail when Shawn Raymond was shot.'

'Jail?' I glanced up at him in surprise. 'Why didn't Gus just tell me that?'

'It's not a secret far as I know. He probably figured it was none of your business. You're not a cop. He's under no obligation to even talk to you, never mind tell you what he considers none of your business – that's the way my brother would think, anyway. Zeke is the family shame. The truth is, Zeke has been in and out of jail – mostly in – for most of his adult life. I was a kid when he went in the first time, and Gus doesn't talk too much about the family felon. Most people don't even know about him. What's strange is that there's a lot of stuff I don't even know about him, about the two of them.'

'There's a lot of space between you and your brothers.'

'I was, as my mother used to say, the miracle of her later years.'

'So Zeke is the bad one and Gus is the good one.'

He nodded. 'It's not as simple as that. What's true is that everything Gus does he has always done from love – toward me, to his kids, to Mattie, to Zeke. "Protect and Serve." Isn't that the motto cops have? Protect and serve, and that's what Gus has always done. Protect and serve, even if it kills you.' He said it sarcastically, nastily, which was something I hadn't seen in him before. 'Gus has always been about that. Protection. Contain and control.'

'I guess that must have plucked his kids' last nerves. That protect-and-serve mess.'

'There's only one kid as far as Gus is concerned.'

'Gina?'

'Lena got more of Gus in her than she did of Mattie. She's as tough as him, as ornery, and there was never any way in hell she was going to let her father control her life.'

'What's Gina like?'

He paused for a moment. 'Very fragile. Let's put it this way – she's been through some stuff in the last year or so that broke her father's heart.'

'Having the baby?'

'That's the least of it, believe me. Did you know she went to Juilliard? She's a musician. She dropped out when she took up with Raymond. The way I understood it, he always kept after her about one thing or another. Mattie says she thinks she had his baby as a "gift" to him. Mattie used to say he just wanted to pull her down to his level. And damned if he didn't.'

'What do you mean?'

'Every dream they had for her he shattered when he met her. Every dollar spent on piano lessons, the good clothes from the expensive stores – all on a cop's salary – all the little Jack and Jill trips and meetings to protect her from "the element" that Gus felt threatened their lives, all of it went right out the window the day she met Shawn Raymond. That along with any self-respect she had. The day Shawn Raymond finally left her alone, the whole family celebrated.'

'Gus said she left him.'

'That's what Gus would like to believe. I'd bet it was the other way around.'

'What exactly did he do to her?'

'Maybe we should call this a business date and we can both add it to our expense accounts,' he added with just enough of an edge to tell me that he meant it.

'Okay then. No more questions,' I said, crossing my heart.

He smiled then and answered me. 'If I knew all the answers, I'd probably tell you,' he added, and I almost believed him.

We finally ordered a light dinner – minestrone and a large Caesar salad – and another round of drinks. He explained in a roundabout way why he hadn't called me again all those years back, and I listened to what he had to say, realizing as he spoke that it didn't really matter too much to me one way or the other anymore. We were both different now – much time and many people had passed between.

I talked about Jamal as I lit into my cheesecake and pulled out the strip of pictures I always carry with me as I sipped my coffee. Ben studied my photos, as interested in them as somebody can be in somebody else's kid, and then talked about his wife and how much he missed her, and how he wasn't sure he could ever love anybody like that again, and I thought about Jake.

I always liked to laugh with Ben Lennox, and we did a lot of it, both of us confessing that we'd probably had too much to eat and drink for a Thursday night. Maybe the ease between us brought on by that last drink was why Shawn Raymond's name came up as he was walking me to my car.

'What I can't understand, Tamara, is why you've gotten involved in this thing in the first place.'

'What do you mean?' Studying him in the light of the parking lot, I had decided that if he wanted to kiss me good night, it wouldn't be such a bad thing at all.

'This whole thing with Shawn Raymond and his junkie mama. Surely you realize by now that you should just let it be. Life served the filthy son of a bitch just what he deserved. I know for a fact that he was nothing but a piece of shit.'

'I thought you said you didn't know him.'

'I didn't,' he said, and kissed me gently on the lips.

Seven

I never do much on Fridays. You can follow your own rhythm when you work for yourself, and my rhythm this day was drag-ass slow. Maybe it was the cumulative effect of staying up late, drinking more wine than I should have, and being more charmed by Ben Lennox than I wanted to admit. I'm enough of a professional to know that it's stupid as hell to get involved with somebody even remotely connected to a case – it can cloud your judgement and make you overlook things you should keep your eye on. Ben's kiss had lingered in my mind longer than it should have, even though I'd been bothered by his parting crack about Shawn Raymond.

On the way to my office that morning, I'd stopped at Dunkin' Donuts and picked up two coffees and a couple of whole wheat doughnuts to push me into gear. Halfway through the second cup, my mind began to function. I settled back in my chair, waited for my computer to boot up, and thought about everything I should be doing. I wrote out my late-as-usual cheque to PSEG, my electric and utilities company, and put the polishing touches on an investigative report I'd done for the personnel department of a bank. Annie had been after me to invest in a larger ad in the commercial section of the telephone book, so I spent a good fifteen minutes playing around with how I should word it. When the phone rang, I ignored it. I could think of at least four people I didn't want to talk to this morning, and I knew that later on I could get the goods on who had called from Karen, the woman who answers my service, who would also put her own unique twist on what they wanted.

When I'd finished playing around with the ad, I went to my working file – YBGB – and jotted down a note at the top of the page reminding me to check on Zeke's stay in jail, and then pulled up my overdue-accounts file and wrote a gently worded reminder letter to a laggard (I myself have been there) about an overdue bill. When the phone rang again, I realized it might be some emergency with my son and picked it up on the first ring.

'Where you been? I been trying to call you for the past hour,' demanded Bessie Raymond, one of those folks I didn't want to hear from.

'Good morning, Bessie. I just got in.'

'Morning! It's damn near afternoon. Steppin' in kind of later, aren't you?'

'Is everything okay?' I ignored her observation about my office hours.

'You find out anything yet?'

'It might take a while, Bessie.' I was beginning to feel depressed about my lack of progress and guilty because of my date with Ben Lennox, which I suspected would make Bessie mad as hell if she knew about it. I wondered again if I'd made a wise decision. I took a fast gulp of coffee, which was cold.

'How long do you think it's going to take?'

'I wish I could tell you, but I just don't know.'

'What you mean you don't know?'

'I told you, Bessie, when I took your case, that I might not have any more luck than the cops did. It might take a while for important things to surface,' I added, hoping to offer some encouragement.

'And here I done gave you all that money!'

'I know you did, Bessie, but there are no guarantees.' 'All that money' wasn't really all that much. 'All that money' was just about gone.

'Did you talk to them Lennoxes?'

'Yes, I did.'

'What did you find out?'

'Nothing new. Mostly the same things they told the police.'

'That they were out on some boat somewhere?'

'You talked to the cops about that too?' Maybe I'd been too quick to judge Osborne for his attitude toward Bessie; apparently he had shared some information with her after all.

'Yeah, I talked to him, for what it was worth. You know I don't trust cops as far as I can spit. You talk to Viola yet?'

'I will next week. Could you tell me a few things about Rayshawn?' I asked matter-of-factly, but felt a sense of dread as I thought about the possibility of telling her the trail to her son's killer could lead straight back to her grandson.

But maybe she knew that already.

'What you want to know about him?' I heard the click of her lighter as she lit up a cigarette and her breath as she pulled it in fast.

'Did you know he has a gun?'

There was a pause before she answered. 'I know his mama's got one.' She didn't ask me how I knew or miss a chance to throw Viola Rudell at me again.

'Bessie, some things have come up-'

'What kind of things?' I could hear the suspicion and distrust in her voice and wondered if I should tell her now about my run-ins with Rayshawn, but then decided against it. If my suspicions about him were right, she'd find out soon enough.

'I'd just like to know more about him. Maybe he knows

something that will help me find out who killed his father,' I said, getting as close as I dared. 'Would you call the Laytons, and ask them if they will talk to me about Rayshawn?'

I heard that lighter click again and the sound of her breath.

'They're good people, them Laytons.'

'I'd like to talk to them. Will you tell them to expect my call?'

She paused so long before she spoke I thought she'd dropped the phone. 'How much time did I buy?'

'As much time as you need,' I said, lying as I said it. She had given me all the money she had, but it would only buy another week at most, and then I'd have to take on something else to pay my bills. I had a son too.

She stuttered out a thank-you before she hung up, and I sat there for a minute or two wondering if I should have told her the truth. The phone rang again, and I let it ring until it stopped, then called my service to talk to Karen.

'How you doing, Ms Hayle' Karen has a pronounced nasal twang that always makes me wonder if I've chosen the best first impression for my struggling business. I have no idea how she looks, but I'm reasonably sure I'd recognize that voice in any crowd.

'Fine, Karen. Got anything for me?'

'Well, this darn phone has been ringing like nobody's business,' she complained, as if I weren't paying her to answer it. 'You got a couple of calls from somebody – Betty Ray or something or other.'

'Bessie Raymond?'

'Yeah. She wouldn't spell her name for me. You better tell that lady that her 'tude is in need of some serious adjustment, somebody better get in there with a wrench or hammer or something and give her mood a tune-up. Anyway, she called about three times. Wouldn't say nothing to me, 'cept her name. Wouldn't even spell—'

I cut her off. 'Thanks, Karen. I've already talked to Ms Raymond.'

'That lady is in need of something only the Lord—'

'Anybody else, Karen?' I asked impatiently.

'No need to snap, Ms Hayle.'

'I'm sorry, Karen. I've got a lot on my mind.' She'd be talking about *my* ''tude' as soon as I hung the phone up.

'Well . . .' She paused as if going through some notes. 'Your girlfriend Annie called. Now that's a lady who got a whole lot of class. You can tell she come from something, not like some of them that be calling you. Said to call her 'cause it was important. And some other lady called but she didn't have a name.'

'Didn't leave a name, Karen?' I cut her off again. 'What did she say?'

'Well,' Karen said, drawling the word out, her own 'tude in tow. 'Real soft voice. Sounded like she was scared of something. Asked for your office hours, I told her what they were. You did tell me I should do that when they asked, right?'

Finally, Gina Lennox had returned my call. 'She just asked for the hours?'

'Just asked for your hours and I gave them to her. Then you got a call from Macy's and another from Visa about those bills you didn't pay,' she said sanctimoniously. I rolled my eyes, wondering why I continued to pay this woman good money to stay in my business and get my messages wrong. 'Then some man called Ben something or other.'

'Ben something or other, Karen?' I asked, truly annoyed. 'Sorry, I didn't mean to snap.'

'That's okay. We all have our days, Ms Hayle. He had a

113

nice voice. Sounded like he was in a hurry, though. Said he'd call you back – at home,' she added suggestively.

'Thank you, Karen. So that was it?'

'That was it. You in for the rest of the day?'

'Yes, probably so. Talk to you later, Karen. Thank you so much for your help,' I added with an unconvincing stab at sweetness.

'That's all right, Ms Hayle. Don't forget to call your friend Annie, and you better get back to them about those bills. They can be right nasty when they want to be. Try to have yourself some fun this weekend. Hope you're feeling better by Monday.' Karen added her own sweet stab.

Despite my annoyance, Karen usually did manage to cheer me up, and I had a smile on my face as I called Annie. But I could tell by her voice that my friend had her own 'tude problem – due, I was sure, to the fact that I hadn't been over to look at her slides and hear about her vacation.

'Half the fun of going somewhere is being able to share it with your best friend when you get back,' she found a way to squeeze into our discussion about a recent meeting of Ujamaa House, a women's organization we both belong to. *Brag about it to your best friend*, I silently substituted, but I knew she was hurt about my not coming over. The truth was, I couldn't think of anything I wanted to 'share' less, seeing that it would be a cold day in Cuba before I had the resources to go on a vacation like that. I had my own attitude about the fact that she should have been sensitive enough to *my* problems to understand that. But friends are friends, so when she mentioned she needed some help cleaning out her garage (her husband William had a bad back and couldn't lift anything heavy without risking a trip to the emergency room), I said I'd help her if I could, and I tossed in Jamal to get back into her good graces.

114

I decided against calling Ben Lennox. After talking to Bessie, I decided to leave well enough alone. I'd call him when I finished up this case, I owed Bessie Raymond that. With her still on my mind, I called the Laytons, leaving a message stating who I was and what I wanted and expressing the hope that Bessie would be in touch with them regarding me. When the phone rang again, I picked it up just in time to make an excuse to Macy's about my bill, which reminded me that I could only give Bessie another week. Looking for answers, I went back into the YBGB file to study my notes, wishing I were making enough money to give the sister more time, wondering if I'd done the best I could do. But the cops had given up on it too. The case was dead cold, and it had probably been foolish and irresponsible of me to get Bessie Raymond's hopes up by letting her think I could do any better. The truth was, I knew now it had been a mistake to take her case in the first place. It had proved to be the lost cause I feared it would be. But I would see it through to the end, and try to give the sister some of what she thought she'd paid for.

The knock on the door when it came was hesitant and uncertain, and I answered it quickly before whoever it was scampered away. Gina Lennox followed me into my office and took a seat in front of my desk like an obedient child.

'I'm sorry to drop in like this, without an appointment or anything, I'm sorry I didn't return your calls,' she muttered in her hushed, little-girl voice. She was dressed in a Black American Princess uniform, subtle and expensive: tiny diamond stud earrings, expensive slacks, tailored silk blouse – no K-mart in sight. I wondered how much longer Daddy was going to pay those bills but realized in the next instant that she was the kind of helpless woman whose upkeep some man would probably contribute to for the rest of her life. I noticed again how thin she was, and despite her well-applied makeup, how

115

drawn and wasted her face looked.

'Thank you for coming.'

'I had to do it for Shawn.' It struck me again how different she was from the way she had looked in that photo. She had lost fire and spirit since her days with Shawn Raymond. I wondered just what that relationship had sucked out of her.

'How's the baby?'

'Fine.'

I cut off my computer and pulled open my notebook, ready to jot down some notes. 'By the way, would you mind giving me his full name again?' Gina looked puzzled, like she wasn't quite sure what I wanted, and then tensed as if she was uncomfortable.

'Augustus Lennox Raymond. After his father and after mine.

'Gus carries Shawn's last name then.'

'Of course.'

'Do you know why his older son, Rayshawn, doesn't carry his name?'

'Because Rayshawn is not his son,' she said with no hesitation.

I put my pen down and looked at her in astonishment. 'Have you ever *seen* Rayshawn Rudell?'

'No, there is no need for me to see him,' she said, her soft voice rising pretentiously, and I liked her less than I had a moment ago.

'No need to see the brother of your son?' I didn't bother to take the sarcasm out of my voice, but she looked so unsettled I didn't push it.

'What exactly did you want to see me about?' She was nervous, and as she crossed her leg her foot hit my desk. I noted that the mere mention of the boy's name seemed to make her edgy.

'I was just hoping you could give me a few more facts about Shawn. You seem a little anxious – could I get you something, some tea maybe?' I offered my usual remedy for anybody – myself included – who has a bad case of nerves. 'I've got herbal, Celestial Seasonings, some Lipton's if you'd like it. Coffee?'

'No. I don't want anything.'

'It's okay if you smoke,' I added, remembering Bessie Raymond, the last nervous person who had sat across from me and how those cigarettes had seemed to calm her down.

A look of disgust crossed Gina's face. 'Why would I want to do that? The smell of them makes me sick. I have never smoked cigarettes in my life,' she added, as if it were a major accomplishment. 'You must have me mixed up with my twin. Lena's the nicotine freak of the family, not me.'

'Lena smokes?' I tried hard to hide my excitement about this new piece of information.

'She used to sneak into the garage and do it when we were teenagers, preteenagers, like thirteen. She has always done a lot of stuff before her time,' she went on, with a smirk that I assumed was supposed to tell me something nasty about her sister's character.

'And you never smoked? Never?'

'No. Why do you keep asking me that?'

'No reason,' I said, shifting my eyes down to my notebook and sitting straight up, like an old dog who just got a whiff of somebody's barbecue. It wasn't Gina in that photo, cigarette and glass in hand, but her twin sister Lena, the smoker. Lena had been playing around with Shawn Raymond too.

'So how did you meet the deceased?'

'Don't call him the deceased. Lena introduced us.'

'How did Lena and Shawn—'

Gina broke in with a feisty defensiveness I hadn't seen before.

117

'Ask her about that. I don't know how she met him. But our families did live close to each other, in the South Ward, the same general area, and he wasn't *that* much older than us in high school. Five years these days isn't that much.'

'Did you go to college after high school?' I needed to place who this girl was, how she lived her life – before and after Shawn Raymond. I noticed she had musician's hands, one of her long tapered fingers adorned by a small diamond that matched the ones in her ears. I remembered what Ben had said about her being a pianist.

'I went to Juilliard for a while. But he was the most important thing to me. He is the only thing that meant anything to me.' She said it with the conviction of someone who has had a religious conversion, light gleaming in her eyes.

'You were studying to be a pianist?'

'That was what my parents wanted.'

'And *you* wanted?'

'Shawn. Why are you asking me about all that?'

'I'm just trying to get as much information as I can. When did Lena meet him?'

'Ask her.' She looked annoyed as she gave me Lena's number, checking first in a small Filofax address book that was in the tiny brown leather bag she carried – which struck me as strange. Even though I call my sister only about once a month, I know her number by heart.

'You and Lena are close?'

'The only person I love more than Shawn and my baby is Lena,' she said so evenly I was sure she was lying. 'And I didn't steal Shawn from my sister if that's what you're thinking. He came to me because he loved me.'

I wished like hell I'd thought to borrow that photo I'd seen over Bessie's. 'Can you think of anything about Shawn that might be helpful?' I went back to my cool, objective voice. Her eyes got a distant look in them before she answered, and she tossed her head up, glancing at the ceiling as if throwing something off, and then her eyes returned to mine.

'Nothing you probably don't know already. He had done a couple of things in his life that were bad, but I understood that and why he had to do them. He got some guns too, you know, from Virginia and sold them up here and in New York.' She paused for a long time, as if she was thinking hard about something, and then she dropped her eyes, avoiding mine. 'He sold some drugs once. He told me about that. He made a lot of money from that, he told me that.'

'Did he ever give you drugs?' I asked, noticing again her thin, frail body, the voice with no body to it.

'No,' she said too quickly, so I knew she was lying.

'You still seem to be in love with him. What finally convinced you to break up with him?'

'That's what I told my parents, because I wanted to live there with them with the baby and all. Shawn really didn't want to live together. I didn't have anywhere else to go.' She glanced down at her hands, which she had folded in her lap like she was sitting in a church choir. 'He wasn't a live-together kind of man, if you know what I mean. But I still went to see him, made love to him whenever I could. I even did it once in their bed.'

'You made love to your boyfriend on your parents' bed?' I kept my voice neutral.

'He said we should,' she said, a mischievous, odd look in her eye.

'But why?'

She shrugged. 'Shawn said it was payback time because my father always treated him like shit.'

'Payback time?'

119

'That was what he said.'

'Your father treated him like shit?'

'That's what he said,' she repeated in the same tone and with no change in her expression.

'So that didn't bother you, making love in your parents' bed. How about him having other women?' I resumed my questioning after a pause, guessing that other women were the least of the situation, and the way her eyes dropped briefly again told me that I'd guessed right.

'No, I didn't care.'

'You're telling me that loving him the way you did, it didn't matter that he had other women?'

'No.'

'How would he have felt if you had other men?'

She shrugged, but the light in her eyes disappeared, and they looked empty for a moment. 'I loved him. I proved that to him anytime he wanted me to. Love means doing what makes the other person happy,' she added pathetically, her voice high and fake, a parody of itself.

'Did you ever talk about trying to have a more, uh, committed relationship?' I tried to take the sarcasm out of my voice.

'I wanted to be whatever he wanted me to be.'

A fool, I said to myself.

'I wasn't ready to force him into anything,' she added.

'Just ready to have his baby,' I didn't bother to conceal the criticism implied by my words.

'I wanted to have his child,' she said, in a voice so filled with emotion I glanced up at her in surprise.

'You knew he had other women yet you never used a condom?' I realised the moment I said it that what the sister did or didn't do with Shawn Raymond and a condom was probably none of *my* business.

'Didn't I just tell you I *wanted* to have his baby?' she snapped, making that point as well.

'Gina, I know you say you loved him, but the man was a self-admitted drug dealer and gunrunner. *Why?* You have so much going for you!'

'Not very much, really,' she said, her voice flat and empty, telling me she believed what she said.

'Could I ask you some questions about your family?'

'You mean like my parents, my sister, my Uncle Zeke?' I got the feeling she was eager to offer him up.

'Let's start with Zeke. Where was he the night Shawn was killed?'

'In jail. He got in trouble once, and he was in jail a long time. He's still on parole. Whenever something happens they pick him up.'

'What did he go to jail for?'

'Robbery and murder.' She said it without flinching, as if it were nothing at all. 'It was no big thing. Shawn did a little time too, he told me.'

And that made it no big thing.

'How long ago was Zeke in?'

'He has been in and out.'

'Would Zeke have had a reason to want Shawn dead?' I asked, and Gina, obviously the mistress of the devil-may-care gesture, shrugged again. But the fact that her eyes wouldn't quite meet mine told me that maybe she believed that *everybody* in her family had a reason to want Shawn Raymond dead. And that could have included her. Lena, at one point in the last year or so, had been partying hearty with her sister's man. Jealousy can run deep between sisters, and I was sure it ran deep between these two. More murderers than a few had loved their victim to death.

121

'Can you think of anybody else who might want Shawn Raymond dead?'

'His old girlfriend, Viola Rudell. She was very very jealous of me and the fact that I had his son.'

'As opposed to the one he didn't own up to? What did Shawn tell you about Viola?'

'That it was over between them.'

'Except for Rayshawn?'

'He never mentioned Rayshawn to me one way or the other.'

'Who do you think killed Shawn Raymond?'

'I told you. Viola Rudell.' Her eyes were big in wide-eyed innocence that didn't fool me. I studied her, a look of exasperation on my face.

'Can you tell me anything else that might be helpful?' She looked puzzled for a moment.

'Gina—'

'I told you all I can,' she said, cutting me off, her face and voice controlled. 'All I will,' she added almost to herself, like an afterthought.

'What was the name of the woman who gave the party, the one you and your sister attended the night Shawn was killed?' At least I could get the name of her alibi if nothing more. She looked startled, like she didn't quite know what I was talking about, then collected her thoughts.

'Claudia. Claudia Holly. She lives in South Orange, off of South Orange Avenue.'

'I'd like to set up a time to see her – would it be all right if I called her? Better still, would you mind calling her and letting her know I'd like to talk to her?' I jotted down Claudia's name. That shrug again, and then a nod as she stood up and prepared to go.

'I've got to get my daddy's car back before it gets too late,' she said as she glanced at her watch. I thanked her for coming, and she left my office. Unsettled by our interview and what I sensed she hadn't told me about her relationship to Shawn Raymond, I stood in front of my window watching her as she left the building and walked toward the parking lot where I had parked my car the night I was held up by Shawn Raymond's son.

It was then that I saw him, laid back in the shadows of the building like he'd been that night, his head tipped to the side as if he was thinking about something that puzzled him, his young body bent slightly and awkwardly like some wizened old man. He watched Gina walk past him, studying her as I studied him. Why had he come back, I wondered, lurking around my office again? Was there something he wanted or needed to tell me?

Rayshawn Rudell.

I thought again about that night and how he had run away at the sound of that one word – son. When I sat back down I called my own son, and because I had no real reason for calling and nothing else to say, I ended up telling him we'd go out that night to his favourite restaurant. We hadn't done Red Lobster together in a very long time. I could almost see the smile pop on his lips. Over the next half an hour or so, I called to make appointments to see Claudia Holly, Viola Rudell, and Lena Lennox, and after some initial hesitation they all agreed to see me. When I looked out the window again to see if Rayshawn was still there, he had gone.

I left the Laytons for last. Bessie had called like I'd asked, and Mrs Layton seemed a nice enough woman, if you could tell anything from her voice, which had a calm, singsong quality to it. I could imagine her talking a scared kid to sleep or quieting the spirit of some troubled teenager over a cup of warm milk in her kitchen. I'd heard a few horror stories about foster parents, but I knew there were a lot of good ones too, and she was obviously one of them.

Rayshawn, she explained, was one of four kids she'd had regularly over the last five years, and my instincts had been right: he had been dropping by her place very frequently since his father's death.

He'd first come into their lives when his mother was doing a stint in a women's prison in South Jersey for passing a bad check, and Bessie, whom she referred to as 'the gran', hadn't been able to take him.

'What about his father?' I asked.

'The gran's son Shawn? He and Rayshawn seemed to get along all right, but about a year ago things started changing,' she explained. 'He stopped taking the boy out, and Rayshawn never seemed to want to see him, but he would come by and visit him, bring money. That kind of thing.'

'So Shawn Raymond was a good father?'

'Well . . .' She paused uncertainly. 'He was so young when Ray was born, couldn't have been more than seventeen or eighteen himself. Too young to be a good father, but he was better than a lot of them.'

'But he did claim the boy as his.'

'All you got to do is look at them together. He wouldn't have needed a blood test to tell him that. But Shawn Raymond was kind of a charmer, a handsome man. Ray is different. He's always been a quiet, moody boy. Even when he was little. Keeps his own counsel, won't tell you nothing unless you push him hard, and I don't. You never know what troubles a child has been travelling with, but they usually find their own way in their own good time, if you let them.'

'What did he say about his father?'

'Not much. It was more in his eyes, the love he had for him.

In his daddy's eyes too, now that I think of it.'

'The love he had for him?' I asked, puzzled.

'Yes, the love.'

'So they had a strong relationship?'

'Well, like I said, about a year ago, Rayshawn started to change. I thought at one point I was going to have to close my door in his face he could get so nasty. He's got a temper on him, slap somebody upside the head, hit somebody, curse somebody out for no good reason. He's not a little boy no more and what comes out his mouth or off his hands is coming from a man's mouth, off a man's fist, not a little boy's. Me and Sam, that's my husband, we're just too old to put up with that mess anymore. I got young kids coming in and out of here who don't need them kind of influences.

'They must have had some kind of fight about something. Shawn Raymond and Rayshawn. That love went out of Ray's eyes. It might have come back, though, if the man hadn't died like he had. A daddy can change things for a boy. Sometimes I wonder what these young souls have done to deserve the kind of burdens they carry.'

'So you see Rayshawn pretty often these days?'

'He comes by here, don't say much of nothing, tries to pick a fight sometimes but mostly he'll just come by, sit, watch something silly on TV, and then go home to his mama, like a little lost ghost.'

'Mrs Layton, do you think Rayshawn could hurt somebody who hurt him badly?'

'That boy has changed so much in this year, I'm afraid he could,' she said, her voice, low like she was telling a secret.

'Do you think it's possible that he could have shot his father?'

'Why do you want to ask me something like that?' She

sounded defensive and protective, and I thought of Bessie Raymond.

'Because I need to know.'

She waited a long time before she answered. 'Kids kill when they ain't got nothing else. That boy didn't have nothing in his life worth living for. His daddy was it and then he disappeared for some reason nobody but God will ever know. I have to tell you the truth, Ms Hayle. When I heard about Shawn Raymond's murder, his son was the first thing that crossed my mind. I thought about mentioning it to the police, but I didn't have proof of nothing. What if I was wrong? You know how these cops always do our boys. I couldn't be part of that. Now, in all honesty, I'm very sure he didn't. I know he loved his father, and I couldn't live with myself if I thought he did something like that and I didn't tell nobody.'

I thought about Rayshawn Rudell and what had been said about him later that night as I sat across from my own son over plates of popcorn shrimp. We were having fun like we always do when we hang out together, mother and son, Tamara and Jamal, against the world.

Jamal had pulled out my chair for me when we sat down, and I thought about Ben Lennox and then Jake when Jamal admitted that he'd seen Jake do that for Denice and Phyllis and it struck him as a cool, respectful thing to do for a woman you cared about.

'Yeah, Jake's a good man to learn from,' I told him, and Jamal nodded his head in agreement as he slurped up the last of his Coke and grabbed for the menu to look at the desserts.

'Have you heard from your father lately?' I asked, as if it had just popped into my mind, not like I'd been thinking about it off and on since I'd said that one word, son, to Rayshawn.

126

'You mean DeWayne Curtis?'

'He's your father, isn't he?'

'If you say so.'

'I don't like the way that sounded, Jamal.'

'I didn't mean to say it like that.' He looked genuinely ashamed, so I let it go.

'You didn't answer my question.'

'About what?'

'Have you spoken to your father recently?' Several years ago, blood precious to both of them had been spilled. I'd never been sure how long it would take Jamal to fully and finally heal.

'No.' He answered sharply with a scowl that was supposed to cut off conversation.

'He hasn't called?'

'I haven't called him back. Can we order some pie now?'

'Do you think you will ever forgive him?' Even as I asked, I knew it was a question for an adult, one he wouldn't be able to answer until he grew up enough to understand that forgiveness doesn't have a hell of a lot to do with the person who has to be forgiven.

'I hate him.' He said it quietly, with an unnerving frankness.

'Do you think we should get some ice cream with our pie?' I asked nonchalantly, like what he'd said didn't matter one way or the other, and he glanced up, relief on his face, glad I wasn't going to push it.

So I ordered the pie and ice cream for both of us and coaxed a smile from him as he devoured my slice. But I couldn't get Rayshawn Rudell or the answer my son had given me out of my mind.

Eight

Another week came and went, and nothing much had changed. I had begun to accept the fact that I probably wouldn't turn up any more than the police had. Then finally came the last week I could give Bessie Raymond. I didn't want to think about that as I drove to work that Monday morning. After several cancellations and reschedulings, I had managed to make appointments to see Claudia Holly, Viola Rudell, and Lena Lennox – all, as it ended up, for that Monday evening. Except for some calls I planned to make during the rest of the week, they were the last loose ends.

I'd also made an appointment that afternoon to meet with a new client, the owner of a small South Jersey janitorial firm who wanted me to go undercover, get chummy with his workers, and sniff out who was ripping him off. He'd already alerted the director of his personnel department that I'd be starting the following week. Ordinarily, hell would have frozen over before I'd agree to scrub out somebody's toilets, but times being tough, those rubber gloves and toilet brushes were sounding pretty good. I'd be based just east of Princeton, far enough away not to run into anyone I knew, close enough to make it to work after having dinner with Jamal. I'd make not only my fee as an investigator but wages as a janitor as well. Every little bit helps.

After lunch, I'd spent an hour or so at Sears picking out a

disguise to wear when I went undercover. I settled on a cheap green polyester pantsuit, which I'd wear with a short grey-streaked wig I'd borrowed from Wyvetta and horn-rimmed glasses. Then I'd spent the rest of the day calling acquaintances in the child protective services, trying to ferret out information on Rayshawn and Viola Rudell, but there was nothing to ferret out.

I headed to Claudia Holly's house a little after six. My office was closer to her place in South Orange than hers was to Shawn Raymond's in Newark, but I clocked it anyway, playing with the idea that maybe Lena or Gina in some wild switch of identities had slipped out of the party, shot Shawn Raymond, and slipped back by the next beat in time to shake a booty. But it was far-fetched, and unless one of them was travelling by *Star Trek* transformer, damn near impossible.

In hasty, messy shorthand, I'd jotted down some routine questions I had for Claudia Holly: How long had she known the twins? How long had they stayed at her house? Could one or the other have made it out and back without anyone knowing? I was also curious about what kind of party she had given – especially on a Thursday night. And I wanted her take – however reluctantly offered – on the twins and their relationship to Shawn Raymond.

South Orange Avenue is a long, wide boulevard that begins in Newark and stretches through several transformations and towns, including the one that bears its name, until it pours into a highway on the top of a mountain. Claudia Holly lived on one of those side streets that used to leave my mouth hanging open when I'd ride down it as a kid. The houses were big and well cared for – broad, lush lawns, neat shrubbery, and shade trees now stripped stark naked by the cold. Except for black folks moving in over the last few years, not much had changed.

The Hollys had probably been among those first black pioneers. Their house at the end of the block was an aged stone Tudor, with diamond-paned, leaded windows and a separate three-car garage. Once upon a time when 'help' was plentiful, cheap, and didn't look like the owners, there had probably been a housekeeper and a groundskeeper too. I double-checked the address before I rang the doorbell, just to make sure I had the right place.

The door was opened by a plump, very light-skinned woman with feathery greyish brown hair who pointed me toward the garage. On closer inspection, I realized it was actually a separate residence, the kind they used to call a mother-in-law apartment, but which now housed a daughter. I approached it across a rough path filled with dead leaves and patches of mud. A willow-thin woman in her twenties dressed in a loose red sweatshirt and black leggings answered my knock.

Claudia Holly was the spitting image of her mother, except her skin was golden brown and her brownish red hair was twisted into tiny, stylish dreadlocks adorned with cowrie shells.

'Tamara Hayle?' she asked with a grin. 'Oh, good. I've always wanted to be interviewed by a private detective.' She was in her mid-twenties, about the same age as Gina, but she moved quickly and talked very fast, and as she bustled me into her home nervous energy seemed to pop from every move. But when we entered the room, I stopped short. Every wall of the large square room was covered with paintings. They were of old neighbourhoods in Newark's Central and South wards: old clubs, factories, and department stores I'd only heard about. There were factory scenes filled with men of all shades and sizes, their angular stylized lunch buckets held at odd angles, their backs bent as they moved past smokestacks. Several pen-and-ink drawings showed children playing jacks on the same

131

sidewalks I'd played on as a child, and there was one breathtaking oil of a woman with a smile so broad and a dress so bright you couldn't pull your eyes away. They were scenes of hope and despair so powerfully executed they literally took my breath away.

'My father's work,' Claudia said proudly, and I realized that she must be the daughter of Claude Holly, a renowned artist who had grown up in Newark's Central Ward and whose death I'd read about in *Jet* a few months before. He was one of those Newark notables always cited in classrooms during Black History Month to remind kids that great men had once roamed the streets they played on. Jake had a print of one of his better-known paintings hanging in his office. I walked toward the paintings in awe, vaguely aware that I'd probably never see them again outside of a museum.

'Daddy's work always has that effect on people,' Claudia said with a nervous laugh.

'It has such power,' I said as I stepped back, taking one last look before I sat down. 'I had no idea you were his daughter.'

'The baby of the family,' she said with a mix of amusement and pride. 'I moved back home when he got sick, to help my mother take care of him, and they fixed up the garage for me. I'm not sure if this is the best environment for his work, but I guess it will be okay until I can find a permanent home for it.' She waved her hand in the general direction of the walls, 'These are what the SoHo gallery I work for calls his "lesser works." But they're important to me . . . How can I help you?' she added as she picked up a glass of white wine and took a sip.

'I'd like to go over what happened the night that Shawn Raymond was shot.'

She looked puzzled for a moment. 'Oh, that happened a long time ago.'

'Yes, it did.'

'You want to know about the guy who used to go with the twins, right? I thought they caught the guy who killed him. I haven't heard anything about it since that cop talked to me right after it happened.' She looked pensive for a moment as she slowly sipped her wine. 'How could I forget it? It was my birthday. Shawn Raymond had the gall to die on my birthday! But I guess everybody has to die on *somebody's* birthday. My father died about a year ago, right around the time Gina's baby was born.'

'Are you close to the Lennox twins?'

'Well . . .' She paused as if she was uncomfortable. 'I care about them and everything, but we've kind of grown in different directions.'

'You were closer when you were younger?'

'We were in Jack and Jill together. That's how I met them. Our mothers were friends, and we're around the same age, but we don't really have that much in common anymore. I'm into my work, art history – I really want to run my own gallery someday. Gina is basically into motherhood and Lena . . .' She paused again, as if trying to think of something to say, then rolled her eyes. 'I think she manages some club on Central Avenue somewhere.'

'So you gave yourself a birthday party the night Shawn Raymond was murdered?'

'It was more like a birthday get-together, and I didn't give it for myself. Lena, Gina, and about half a dozen of my friends who knew I'd been depressed about my father's death came by after work to cheer me up and brought over a big basket of foods they knew I like: champagne – the good stuff – some freshly baked baguettes, Brie, English cheddar, pâtés, cake. We all gorged ourselves like pigs. It was really fun. Then the next day Gina found out Shawn had been murdered.'

'So the party was the Lennox twins' idea?'

'By way of Mattie, probably. You know Mattie, their mom? Mattie is always doing thoughtful things like that. She's the kind of woman who remembers everybody's birthday, which I never do. I think Lena said something about her mother mentioning that they should surprise me and cheer me up on my birthday, so she did. Nice, huh?'

'Very nice. Especially since you all weren't that close. So Gina and Lena were both here until two in the morning?'

'Definitely.'

'You sound very sure about that.'

'Gina wanted to get back to breast-feed her baby, and she said it was around two because her breasts were starting to leak. It struck me as weird that a mother could actually tell time by her breasts, so I remembered the time that she said.'

'Is there any way that one of them – Gina or her sister – could have slipped out without—'

A look of annoyance crossed Claudia's face as she interrupted me. 'Dressed in each other's clothes like in a B movie? Run out, shoot the fool, and make it back in time to sip champagne? Come on, Tamara – is that what you said your name was? You've got to do better than that!' It did sound dumb, and I wished I hadn't mentioned it. I shifted through my notebook, pretending to look over my notes.

'No, nobody left,' she said with a trace of condescension. 'Unless you want to count the fifteen minutes Gina ran out to pick up some ice before the liquor stores closed.'

'Around ten?'

'Yeah, and she came right back. Yeah, I remember the time because Lena kept making a big thing about it, telling her to forget about it because it was too late and the stores would be closed. But Gina went anyway.'

'So she left at ten and made it back by ten-fifteen?'

Claudia looked perplexed for a moment, 'Yeah, I guess, around then. She came back, I know that, because Lena was so worried about her getting back right away. It was ten-fifteen, almost exactly.'

'You told the cop about that?'

'I'm sure I did,' she said, too quickly. 'I know I did,' she continued uncertainly.

'Do you remember how the twins were dressed?'

'Are you back to that? God, no!' Claudia said, putting her hands over her face. 'Come on, this happened six, seven months ago.'

'Do you remember what they talked about?'

'Hell if I know! You're asking too many questions! Do you actually think Gina or Lena killed the asshole?'

I smiled and backed down a little. 'When I first mentioned Shawn you said he was "the guy who used to go with the twins." Did you mean twins or twin?'

'I meant what I said,' she said with no change of expression.

'So obviously they both were getting it on with Shawn Raymond, right?' She shrugged, sipping wine as I continued. 'And usually when that's the case, knowing what I know about men, women, and sibling rivalry, somebody's nose is out of joint.'

'Believe me, you've got that wrong. Yes, they were both "getting it on," as you put it, with Shawn Raymond. I guess there's no reason to keep that particular piece of information confidential now that the man, such as he was, is dead.'

'How did you feel about Shawn Raymond? He was a good-looking brother and obviously had your two friends enthraled.'

'Me?' She wrinkled up her nose as if she'd just smelled

something unpleasant. 'I don't like to speak ill of the dead, especially since my friend loved him.'

'You mean friends.'

'I said friend as in *one* friend and *loved*. Let's put it this way. My girl Lena took Shawn Raymond about as seriously as he took her, which was about as seriously as Lena takes everything in life, which is not very seriously at all. To hear Lena tell it, Shawn Raymond was a good fuck, spent good money, and knew how to show a girl a good time when she felt like having one. What more can you ask of a man?' She winked mischievously.

'And what was he to Gina?'

'The man was like a drug to Gina. An honest-to-God, snorting, shooting, drag-your-ass-through-the-mud drug. Gina was a serious Shawn Raymond fiend.'

'How did you feel about him?' I went back to my original question.

'I thought he was kind of a sleazebag if you want to know the truth. Kind of a lowlife. I don't associate with people like Shawn Raymond.'

'People who . . .' I waited for her to fill in the blanks.

'Do the kind of stuff he did, a little shady, a little slick, a little fast, but fine, if you like a man who moves and dresses like he's a car chase ahead of the mob. I think he grew up kind of underprivileged.

'I'm really not ashamed of being middle-class,' she added, as if I had suggested that she should be. 'I'm privileged, I've always been privileged, I know it. I had good parents and on and on and on. My dad was famous. The dads of all my friends are kind of semifamous – like Mr Lennox, you know, he was like a famous police officer and everything.'

'I heard. And Shawn Raymond?'

'Lena told me his father was murdered when he was a baby. Wow, that's like father like son – I just thought about that!' she added, widening her eyes. 'And he grew up in a very bad inner-city neighbourhood, you know the spiel. The reality is, a guy like Shawn Raymond should probably never have even crossed Gina's or Lena's or *my* path in life, for that matter.'

'But for . . .?'

'Well, my mom said that if Mr Lennox had just gotten them out of Newark when he should have, they probably wouldn't have ended up with a man like that.' I guess she must have noticed the look on my face, because she backtracked quickly. 'Well, I'm not saying that there is anything wrong with Newark, but if they had left—'

'Left Newark?' I snapped, Newark pride shining through.

'I mean, I'm down with the brothers and sisters in the hood and everything. And it's not like there aren't any nice neighbourhoods in Newark, like over near where the twins lived. My father grew up in Newark, in the Central Ward – look, everything he painted was Newark.' She pursed her lips. 'Well, all I'm trying to say is, she had a lot going for her, and she ended up with Shawn Raymond and she probably wouldn't have if she'd gone out with some of the guys we knew in Jack and Jill.'

'Gina's problems have absolutely nothing to do with growing up in or dating guys from Newark. I grew up in Newark,' I added, with what I hoped was dignity but with more of a defensive edge in my voice than I meant to put there.

'Sorry!' she said, only slightly embarrassed.

'What are they like, Gina and Lena?' I asked, cooling down my civic pride.

'Gina is naive. He was just bad for her in every way a man can be for a woman.'

137

'Did he ever hit her?'

'Well, there are more ways to hit a woman than with your fists,' she said, and I flinched inwardly as I thought about my own relationship with DeWayne Curtis, my ex-husband, who had never laid a hand on me, but when I left him I was about as battered as a woman can be.

'Did Gina know that her sister was involved with Shawn Raymond?'

Claudia sighed as if she were letting out some bad air. 'She knew it but she didn't know it, if you know what I mean. Gina is one of those women who don't like to face things. Shawn could have done some hoochie on the foot of the bed, and she would have rolled over to the other side and gone back to sleep. Gina doesn't see things she doesn't want to see.'

'Was Gina mad that her sister was involved with Shawn Raymond?' I rephrased the question and asked.

Claudia dismissed it with a shrug and a toss of her head. 'All I know is, one day Shawn Raymond was just there, looking good, talking shit, and messing up *both* those women's lives.'

It was dark when I headed back to Newark by way of South Orange Avenue, and the city was showing its age. Although the distance from Newark wasn't far in miles, it was in everything else. The streets were nearly empty as I got closer to the heart of the city, and folks kept their eyes to themselves and their pace quick. For the hell of it, maybe because Gina's attitude toward my hometown had pissed me off more than I wanted to admit, I drove by the block where I grew up. I slowed down as I passed the spot where the riots started, tasting again the acrid bite of the tear gas in the back of my throat, and feeling the dread I'd felt that night as I waited for my father to come home through the throng of white men who had lined the street like an occupying army to 'protect' the citizens from themselves. I thought about Pandora. I hadn't been that much older than her when everything went down. I thought about Rayshawn and his father, Shawn, and *his* father, Antoine, and what the city had ended up serving them. I remembered again the Shawn I'd known – all skin and bones and pretty eyes, grown up to be a man who would break a father's heart.

What would my brother have thought of him now?

Two men sitting on the stoop watched me as I got out of my car and walked toward Viola Rudell's building. I could tell one was high, and I felt the eyes of the other on me as I strutted my tough-girl strut up the stairs, daring someone to say something. I rang the doorbell, and heard him move toward me, and then felt his hand on my arm. I could smell his liquor breath and feel it against the side of my face. The leer on his face turned my stomach. I pulled my arm away roughly, and moved away from him, quickly glancing around to see if there was anyone else on the street. Suddenly a woman, not much taller than a kid, came striding down the hall, glaring at him through the barred door as she approached. He stepped back to return to his perch on the step, muttering curses to his partner.

'Viola Rudell?' I asked her, and she nodded, her eyes shyly avoiding mine as she led me back up the hall and into her apartment. Wind chimes hanging on the back of the door tinkled as she closed it, and the scent of jasmine hung sweet and heavy in the air.

'It gets to smelling so bad in here I've got to burn something,' she said, explaining the odour. Her voice had a deep, tender edge to it, as sensual in its own way as the smell of the incense. The apartment was tiny and narrow, and I noticed that the door to a bedroom down the hall was partly open. I wondered if Rayshawn was home, then realized that if he were, it would probably be closed. A sweater, which was obviously his, hung on the doorknob, and a large sneaker lay on the floor. The sag and uneven stuffing of the worn gray tweed couch where we sat told me that it was probably a sleeper, and the comfortable way Viola slipped off her shoes and curled them under the blanket that lay on top of it told me she slept here, giving her son the bedroom, doing the best by him that she could.

I studied her face closely in the overhead light that dimly lit the room. She was strikingly pretty, with clear, even brown skin and long-lashed eyes with a slant to them, sloe-eyes. Her hair was short and close to her head, which gave her face a funny, elfish look, like that of a charming but mischievous child. Rayshawn took after her in build; she too was slight, not that much larger than her son.

'I'm little, I always been little, so I learned to fight early,' she said quietly, as if answering my unasked question about the reaction to her of the men on the porch. 'The two of them sitting out there know I can kick their doped-up asses anytime I set my mind to it,' she added, with a mixture of pride and fierce bravado that sounded like a kid and made me smile. I took out my notebook and opened it, but quickly closed it when she glared at me suspiciously.

'You a cop?'

'No.'

'Then why you got to take notes?'

'I don't have to.'

'I don't want nobody knowing what I say or do.'

'Are you afraid of something – someone?' I wondered about the hint of worry that had come into her eyes.

'There ain't nobody in this world I'm afraid of anymore.'

'Were you afraid of Shawn Raymond?'

'I knew him since he was going on twelve. How am I going

to be afraid of a man I knew as long as that? But they took him away the way they take away everything I love, everything I got.' She spat the words out defensively.

'Who, Viola?'

There had been a markedly paranoid note in her voice, and her shrug was self-conscious. She had an odd, secretive look on her face that told me she wasn't saying everything that was on her mind.

'Could you tell me about him?' I softened my tone and leaned toward her, letting her know I was eager to listen to whatever she wanted to tell me.

She paused as if she was thinking about what I'd just said before she spoke. 'He busted my cherry. I guess you could say I handed it to him when I was going on thirteen. He wasn't all that much older, a year and a half, maybe two.' She smiled strangely to herself, as if recalling some forgotten, bittersweet memory that she didn't want to share. 'I had a lot of men come and go through my life, but there was always Shawn. Always.'

'Were he and your son close?'

She glanced up quickly, her eyes wary. 'My son Rayshawn? Yeah, they were close. Until that bitch Shawn was going with had that baby – things changed some after that.'

'What can you tell me about Gina Lennox and Shawn?'

She looked at me blankly for a moment and then her eyes left mine and fastened on the incense. 'What you want to know? I knew about all Shawn's bitches,' she said, a dismissive chuckle coming from deep within her throat.

'Were they in love?'

'Hell, no.'

'She thought they were.'

'She'd do anything he said to do, didn't matter what it was. A man like Shawn couldn't love a woman like that. He couldn't

141

love a woman who showed no respect for herself. She was a joke to him, except for that baby.'

'How did you feel about her?'

'Shawn Raymond is dead because of that rich bitch Gina Lennox. I say that out loud to myself and to my boy a hundred times a day. I know it in my soul, that Shawn is dead because of her. Don't ask me how I know it, but I do.'

'Who do you think killed him, her or somebody in her family?'

'Them hincty niggers over there off Bergen?' She glanced down, shaking her head hopelessly. 'I don't know.'

'What about Lena Lennox?' I asked, just for the hell of it.

'Lena who? I never heard of no Lena Lennox. Gina had two names?'

I searched her face, wondering if she was joking, but it was clear that she wasn't. Lena Lennox was obviously one 'bitch' Shawn hadn't told her about. I went back to the sister she knew. 'So things changed between you and Shawn after Gina had her baby.'

She settled back against the couch, staring at the incense, and then sucked her teeth and threw her head back in a gesture of pride touched with defiance. 'You know Shawn was a kid himself when Rayshawn was born. I was how old – fourteen maybe, going on fifteen? Sometimes having a baby for a man is all a young girl who don't have nothing else going for her thinks she can do. He was seventeen when I had Rayshawn. We didn't have no business having a kid, but we did, and Shawn was the only kind of father a boy that age can be.'

'Did he turn his back on Rayshawn when Gina had her baby?' I asked, my voice sympathetic.

She stared at the half-open door of her son's room for a while without saying anything, as if she could see him or wanted to, and there was a tired, defensive edge in her voice when she spoke. 'He loved her baby because he was part of him, not because of her. He was carried away by that baby, that was all, the way some men get carried away sometimes. Played around with being a father like he couldn't do before, when we had Rayshawn. It's easy to love a child when they're little. But they sure grow up, don't they, then all you got is what you raised, staring you up and down, ready to spit in your face. You got any kids?' Her dark eyes fastened on me, searching my face.

'Yes, I have a son.'

'What's his name?'

'Jamal.'

'Oh, that's a pretty name. Sounds so soft and gentle.' Her voice was soft and gentle as she said it. 'You with his daddy?'

'No.'

'How old is he?'

'A little older than yours. Not much older, though.'

'A little man, huh?' She grinned.

'He thinks so.'

We both laughed at that, the way mothers do when they have nothing else in common. She watched the incense for a while and neither of us said anything until she broke the silence in a flat voice.

'Is Bessie paying you to find out who killed him?' I told her that she was, and she laughed disdainfully.

'You having any luck?'

'No.'

'She thinks I killed Shawn.'

'Did you?'

Her eyes turned hard and empty, but then they softened. 'You think I'd hurt the only thing I loved besides my son?'

'Where were you the night he was murdered?' I asked, knowing that it had probably been asked and answered before.

'I told the cops.'

'Please tell me.'

'Here with Rayshawn. She lit another stick of incense and waved it around, and the room filled again with its smell. 'It stinks in here so bad I can't stand it sometimes. It smells dirty no matter what I do, like some dirty something or other came in here when I was out and peed on the floor. Nasty, that's the way it smells. The incense makes it smell nice when it burns like this. Like it used to smell in church when I was a kid.'

'Did Shawn ever mention somebody named Chee-chee to you?' I asked her now, watching her carefully for the betrayal of any emotion or hidden truth. Her face relaxed, and she breathed in the smell of the room as if it were a drug.

'You talking about Chee-chee? That old dude used to hang around? Shawn used to get sick of his old-ass, doped-up self, always trying to score some drugs.'

'Do you know where he lived?'

'Shawn never said too much about him, except they went back, way back.'

'Is that all?'

'What more was there to say? He wasn't nothing but an old drugged-up nigger who got on Shawn's nerves, that was all.'

I began to gather up my things. But before I left I threw out my last question, the one that had nothing to do with why I was here but that had nagged at me, scared me from the moment I'd heard the story.

'Could you tell me one thing, Viola?'

'Didn't I answer everything you wanted to know about Shawn?'

'It's not about Shawn.'

'What's it about then?'

'Why did you put that scar on that girl's face?' Viola looked startled for a moment, and then dropped her head like she was ashamed. But when she picked it up again, there was a smile on her face so slight I wasn't sure it was there until she spoke.

'Why don't you ask the bitch who wears it?'

'Viola Rudell was the only woman Shawn made me promise to stay away from. He always used to say she was very good with a knife,' Lena Lennox told me with a little chuckle about an hour later when, still in Newark, I sat across from her. She looked amazingly like her sister, but she'd added a tiny gold nose stud in her left nostril since the photo, and it gave her an exotic, East Indian look. Her voice was deeper and richer than her sister's, and the bright red of the loose caftan she wore was as much her colour as it hadn't been Gina's. I'd heard that one twin is always dominant – smarter, faster, stronger, the one who battles for and wins the bigger share of nutrients in the womb. In the case of these two twins, it was clear who the winner was.

'Why would he tell you that?'

'If you've met her, which I'm sure you have, that should be obvious.'

'Did you know she cut up a woman's face?'

Lena shuddered. 'No, I hadn't heard that. Very good with a knife, right? That was typical of Shawn, to say something like that, and have his disgusting little joke.'

'What do you know about her son, Rayshawn Rudell?'

'Nothing, except he's as violent and brutal as his mother. Shawn and I ran into him a couple of times when we were together. He pulled a gun on Shawn once. This was maybe a month after we started hanging out, before he started with Gina.

We were coming home from a club and this kid – he couldn't have been more than ten or eleven – suddenly attacks him on the street, screaming and crying and hitting him with his hands, something about his mama. It was the first time I knew he had a kid, and the level of the boy's rage scared me shitless. Shawn did nothing, and he didn't even look upset. He showed nothing, not fear, not anger, not concern, just nothing at all. When the kid pulled the gun out, I don't think he was going to use it, he just pulled it out, almost like he was proud of it, to show it to Shawn, and Shawn just took it from him, and just told him to keep his hands out of his business. He was very matter-of-fact about the whole thing.'

'What did you think about that?'

'I didn't think anything about it. This may sound weird, but I always just thought Shawn was kind of, well, wild, dangerous. He was obsessed with guns, and I found that and everything else about him kind of erotic. I guess I was as stupid as my sister is.'

'Of everyone he was involved with – you, Gina, Viola Rudell – who do you think Shawn loved?"

'That's easy. Himself.' She reached for a cigarette, quickly lit it, and then sucked on it leisurely. 'Do you actually think at this point you will find out something about Shawn's death that the cops can't?'

'I don't like to give up.'

'Suit yourself then.' She blew smoke rings out over her head in a dismissive gesture.

'Did Shawn ever mention somebody named Chee-chee to you?'

She looked surprised, taken aback. 'How did you find out that name?'

'Heard it around.'

146

'Chee-chee was what Shawn used to call my Uncle Zeke.' I was stunned for a moment but got it together fast.

'So Chee-chee is Zeke Lennox. Where did the name Chee-chee come from?' I asked, eager to get as much as fast as I could, and this was one question answered, for what it was worth.

'I guess it was from Uncle Zeke liking to do so much dope. Maybe after cheba-cheba, this dope I heard they used to smoke during the sixties, or Cheech and Chong, those guys who did the marijuana movies. That was where that name came from.'

'So you met Shawn through your Uncle Zeke, Chee-chee?' I ventured a guess.

Lena chuckled and blew out a trail of smoke. 'I used to partake of the weed – still do occasionally – and of anything else I could get my hands on, and my uncle was the biggest druggie going. He knew how to get drugs and I wanted to get some and that led me to Shawn and I eventually led him to Gina and that is the story of how I led the family favourite, my do-no-wrong virtuous twin, into the hands of the evil seducer – in a nutshell.'

'Your do-no-wrong virtuous twin?'

'If you met my father you know what I'm talking about. But I am Uncle Zeke's favourite,' she said, with a smirk that told me at once about her relationship to her uncle and her place in the family.

'So you two are the family secrets, in a manner of speaking?'

'In a manner of speaking.'

'It's obvious why your father was ashamed of Zeke, with his drugging and incarceration and all, but what about you?'

'Have you met Gus Lennox?' She lit up another cigarette, smoking like Bessie Raymond this time, pulling the smoke into her body fast and blowing it out in the same rush of anger and frustration. 'I could never be what he wanted me to be. He could never control me, and I am a control freak's worst nightmare. Completely *out* of control.' She shook her head and started to laugh, but it sounded false.

'Everybody wonders what Gina saw in Shawn, let me tell you what she saw. She saw our father – Augustus Lennox. The same aggressive nothing-but-me-means-anything shit, the same foul mouth and ugly manner, the same rigidity. Gina was fucking our father for Christ's sakes. She became whatever Gus wanted her to be, and she looked for a man who would do her the same favour.'

'And what about you, Lena? Who were you fucking?' I asked it like I did to shock her more than anything else, to see what her reaction would be. She seemed to have considerable insight into her sister; I wondered if she had any into herself.

She looked amused when she answered. 'I guess I was fucking him too, right? For different reasons, though – to get even, to do my hating on my own terms. I liked fucking Shawn. To have him on my own terms. To be completely in control. Like father, like daughter.'

'So you hated Shawn Raymond, and that was why you kept sleeping with him?' I asked her doubtfully, recalling the photograph of the two of them, the laughter in her eyes.

She was pensive for a moment. 'Not at first. He was different at first, and honest in a funny kind of way. Completely honest about his lack of feeling, or anything decent for that matter. We had a connection. He didn't give a damn about anybody or anything and neither did I. We played chicken with each other's feelings. Fun, huh? He couldn't touch me because nobody can. I guess I have Gus Lennox to thank for that.'

'Was your father sexually abusive?' That had occurred to me when I'd watched Gina in my office, and it had sent a chill

148

through me then and did now, because it would explain one daughter's subjugation and the other's rage. Couple that with a cold, compulsive mother who, from what I had seen when I visited them, seemed to be the kind of woman who cleaned her house, cooked her meals, and neither saw nor spoke evil because she didn't like to rock the boat.

'No, he certainly was never that.'

'He was emotionally abusive?'

'You could probably say that.'

'In what ways?'

'It's hard to explain except that you never knew when you would do something wrong, and the payback he gave you – the slaps, the shouts, the derision, made you feel like shit afterwards, like you didn't deserve to live. Some people who don't know anything about raising kids might say he was just a very strict disciplinarian. You had to do exactly what he said. He gave you no room to breathe, to be who you were.'

I recalled what Ben had said about his brother and the shadow that passed over his eyes when he mentioned him. And I thought about my relationship with my own mother, whose slaps and screams always seemed to come from nowhere with no reason or warning. It was the thing that I had sensed about Gus Lennox that afternoon, the thing that had clawed deep in my gut.

'So you always did what he said?' I asked, knowing that she probably had, like I had. But her laughter surprised me.

'Hell, no! I *never* did. But Gina! Always. Until Shawn Raymond. Shawn was Gina's one big rebellion. Her one chance at defiance. And you see what that got her.'

'What did it get her?'

Her face went blank, and her eyes grew dark with distress. She was quiet for so long that for a moment I thought she was dismissing me, ending our interview for some reason she didn't want to explain. But then she spoke, in a low, harsh whisper, almost as if she wanted to make sure nobody else would hear her.

'Shawn got her started on rock, and then he made her do . . .' She paused, as if trying to get the words out. 'He made her do disgusting things to prove that he could do it, that he could take somebody as innocent as Gina, as fucking dumb as Gina, who thought she loved him so much, and make her do something humiliating just to prove that he had that much power over her, that she belonged to him.'

'What kind of things did he do?'

'He made her fuck his friends,' Lena muttered, with such a look of revulsion on her face I thought she might be sick. 'They were just some dumb, low-life niggers he knew from nowhere, who shared his booze or his ride or his drugs, so he let them share his "bitch", and the thing I could never forgive her for was that she let him do it. She actually did it. And he told me about it, bragging about it to me, like my sister wasn't shit, like I would think it was funny that he could turn my sister into a junkie whore like his mama had been. He talked about how he made her go down on these dudes, down on the floor on all fours, like the dog he liked to call her.'

She began to cry at the memory of her sister's shame, her body shaking hard and her nose running like a little girl's. She pulled herself together after a moment or two, cleared her throat and began again.

'I told Daddy about it, though. I hadn't spoken to him in a year and a half, but I called him up, the first time it happened, and I went over the house and I told him. I had to tell him that shit because I hoped he would do something about it, and then he went to Shawn and told him that if he didn't leave her alone, leave us alone, he would kill him.

'Gina was pregnant by then with the baby, and my parents went and got her out of this shitty hole he had her stuck up in, and cleaned her up and brought her home and told her that as long as she didn't see Shawn again, she could stay there until she broke her habit and got on her feet.'

'But she started seeing him again?' It was a question I knew the answer to.

'Yeah.' She picked up a cigarette and smoked it down, and we didn't speak again until she finished. 'I'm just glad the bastard is dead. My sister would be better off dead too.'

I left Lena's place, went home, and took a shower, washing Shawn Raymond off of me, feeling as if he had reached up from the grave to touch me with his dirt, as Gus Lennox had put it that time at his house. I couldn't get Lena's story about her sister out of my mind, or what Bessie Raymond's son had done.

Over the rest of the week, I made the calls I needed to make – to Osborne, to verify that Zeke had been in jail, to Mrs Layton again, to talk some more about Rayshawn, and to Viola, to see if there was anyone else who could verify that she was home when Shawn was killed. I avoided Bessie Raymond, and when she finally got through, cigarette probably dangling in her mouth, grief bursting in her voice, I put her off with vague promises about a written report within a week or so that would detail my expenses and explain exactly how I had spent her money.

I did run through various scenarios in my mind for the hell of it, making sure I had covered any possibilities: that Lena and Claudia had conspired to kill the man out of revenge; that Gina, finally straight, understood what he had done to her, and sometime in that fifteen or twenty minutes when she'd gone to get the ice, had found a way to get to him, stick around until midnight, and shoot him out of rage; that someone had gotten Zeke – Chee-chee – out of jail and he'd done it for the hell of it; that Viola was lying for Rayshawn or Rayshawn was covering for his mother. But I knew that nothing made any sense. The cops had had it right from the first: everybody was somewhere else with somebody else when it happened.

And maybe he just deserved it.

So Bessie Raymond had paid me all that money and wouldn't find out squat. I'd write my report, send it to her certified mail, and call it a day.

Had I paid my brother's debt?

Damned if I knew one way or the other.

Nine

And maybe he deserved it.

That thought stayed in the back of my mind whenever I sat down to do my final report for Bessie Raymond and couldn't seem to write it. I didn't want to tell her everything I knew about her son. He was dead now – what good would it do? *She could have helped Shawn turn himself around, helped him make himself into somebody*, Bessie had said about Gina that first day in my office. But he had brought her down, and I knew that would shame Bessie in ways nothing else could.

I hadn't decided what I was going to say about her grandson either. I had my suspicions about Rayshawn Rudell, but that was all they were, and the more time that passed the less I believed them. I probably should have gone to the police about that gun and his attempted robbery and lodged a formal complaint against him the day it happened. But I hadn't been able to do it. Maybe because I believed that he deserved another chance and, like Bessie Raymond, don't trust cops worth spit when it comes to dealing with young black men. I'd seen them in action when I was on the force, and off it. I was sure I could find another way that wouldn't mark the boy for life with a record. I know how the criminal justice system chews up and spits out kids who look like my son, and I didn't want to be the one to shove that last rusty shiv into Bessie Raymond's weary back. Maybe I didn't do it because I'm nothing but a damn fool.

So I kept putting off writing that report, and it just sat in my computer. There were days I was just too tired to do it. All that scrubbing and grinning at the janitorial company did take its toll. Half the time, I didn't make it into my office at all during my free time. I did talk to Jake about looking into the possibility of getting Rayshawn into a residential programme for troubled teenage boys, and he'd found one that would take him down near the Pennsylvania border. He also found a lawyer who would help Bessie Raymond secure grandparent visitation rights. All that made me feel better.

And finally I heard from Osborne.

'Uh. Mizz Hayle? They think they got the guy who killed – uh – Shawn Raymond,' he said in his dull monotone. 'One of his own kind.'

'His own kind?' I asked defensively, always suspicious of the stereotypes cops hold about black folks.

'The gunrunnin' kind.' he snapped, perhaps sensing my suspicion. 'A kid.'

'How old a kid?' I'm not sure why I asked, except I heard the word 'kid' and thought of my own.

'A kid past the age of consent so we don't have to bother with that juvey nonsense. Eighteen, nineteen? I don't know. A kid who lives in Virginia.'

'Why are they so sure it was him?'

'This kid was packing a .38 for one thing. Same kind of slug killed Raymond. Him and Raymond had some kind of beef about the business they were doing, was the word on the street. They fell out, and he did him. Kid's a felon from way back.'

'Does this kid have a name?' I don't know why I asked that either, except he was some mother's son.

'A name? How the hell am I supposed to know that? Some nameless kid, that's all. Shawn Raymond was dealing guns, transporting them up from VA, right? One of his junior partners didn't like something he was doing, came up, and took him out, right? One. Two. Three. Pop. Took him out with a piece of the merchandise. The usual shit. No big thing.'

Black men killing black men. So nobody gives a good goddamn.

'Why are they so sure that he is the one?' I was still doubtful.

'Didn't I just tell you the kid was a felon?' Osborne snapped impatiently. 'Been in and out of jail since he was thirteen years old. Jesus H. Christ, that should tell you something right there. So he hit the big time with this one. Murder one. Manslaughter. He's in the big league now. They're trying to squeeze a confession out of him as we speak.'

'And they are sure?'

'You got any better ideas?' I had to admit that I didn't.

'I talked to his mother, Mrs Raymond, as soon as I heard,' he added almost contritely. 'She seemed to accept it,' he threw in as if he wanted to convince me too, although he didn't need to bother. It actually did make sense. A sad, tragic sense. Another kid who hadn't had a chance gone down. I thanked him for his help, told him I was glad that things had been resolved, and with that brief conversation, things were brought to a close. Maybe I could let it go.

Finally, after all my procrastinating and avoiding Bessie's calls, I was able to put the finishing touches on my report, explaining exactly how I had spent her money (I didn't include the manicure), apologizing for what I hadn't been able to find out, but pointing out that her involvement may have sparked the cops' renewed interest in the case. I included the name of the lawyer that Jake had given me as well as the contact for the program for Rayshawn. I also warned her in strong language that Rayshawn had been on the verge of committing a serious felony and had some serious problems that had to be dealt with, and that if she and Viola didn't make sure he got help, I'd be forced to go to the authorities with information that would result in his arrest.

Bessie called a week later to thank me and say she had spoken to Osborne and was feeling much better, and that she had contacted the pro bono lawyer. She had also convinced Viola to place Rayshawn in the centre, but they wouldn't be able to take him until spring. So that was the end of it. I was finally able in good conscience to let it go. A burden had been lifted.

Ben Lennox called me at home the Saturday after my talk with Bessie and I agreed to go out for a drink with him. Since my janitorial work took up my nights, we started meeting for lunch, and then over the next few weeks, for weekend dinners. I began to look forward to our dates. He was still depressed about his separation from his wife, but I knew our relationship was important to him.

A month of casual dates had passed before I realized that he made me laugh when I didn't feel like laughing, and I always felt better about myself and the world after I'd left him. I looked forward to talking to him each morning after a hard night of scrubbing floors. I hadn't introduced him to Jamal yet. I've always felt that meeting my son was an honor, not a privilege, so I've never brought men into his life who I didn't think would be there for a while. Jamal was getting curious, though, and I knew the time was near.

Ben never mentioned Gus, and I often forgot that he was the reason for our renewed connection. He spoke of Gina and Lena only in passing, and it was easy to think of them as the little girls he remembered and forget what I knew about them as women. I never mentioned what Lena had told me about Gina, but I was sure he knew the story. I saw it in the way his eyes glazed over with hatred the one and only time Shawn Raymond's name slipped into the conversation.

I'd seen Gus Lennox only once since Ben and I began dating. Ben had stopped by his house one night to pick up some papers, and I'd come inside with him to wait. Gus had watched me warily, clearly uncomfortable in my presence. Ben seemed to enjoy his discomfort, which I found oddly reassuring. My presence in Ben's life seemed to give him the courage he needed to stand up to his brother, to be his own man around him, and I liked giving him that.

We hadn't slept together yet – this time around. I've evolved into the kind of woman who is slow in deciding when to make love to a man – fast, bad choices have taught me that anything worth having is worth waiting for. But our kisses were longer and more passionate and his touches more lingering. And I found myself remembering that time we'd made love. Ours was not a hot fast desire, but an easy, slow-burning one, the kind that if tended with care just might last a lifetime. I hadn't felt that for a man – an *available* man – in a very long time.

So when Ben invited me to Gus Lennox's house for dinner on Mattie's birthday, I gladly accepted. I was now reasonably sure that Gus had nothing to do with Shawn Raymond's death, and I was ready to make a new start with his family. Ben clearly had a complex, difficult relationship with his older brother, which had played a role in destroying his marriage. But I've had my share of complex, difficult family relationships, and I fully understood. By the time the Wednesday of the party rolled around, I'd managed to forget my misgivings about his two brothers and was prepared to face them in a different, kinder frame of mind.

157

My janitorial job had ended that Monday. The cops had arrested the thief – an unpleasant jerk who spent his time talking trash to his female co-workers, and I'd been only too glad to get the goods on the fool. For appearance's sake, I'd stayed on another week. The owner was so pleased with my work he'd given me a generous bonus as well as the promise of a strong recommendation whenever I needed one. So I was ready to party that Wednesday. I took half of my bonus and treated myself to a new dress (on sale), and that morning stopped by Wyvetta's for a touch-up (that wig had done a number on my hair) as well as a manicure – even letting Lucy have her way with my nails and a polish called Hot Pepper Red. When night fell, I felt like a hot red pepper.

We got to the party around nine. Mattie, groomed and perfumed, was dressed elegantly for an evening at home – black velvet jumpsuit, casually set off with simple silver-and-onyx earrings. She led us into the large living room, which was gaily decorated with silver helium balloons and a white and pink and silver 'Happy Birthday' banner plastered across the wall. She was far more relaxed than she'd been our first time around, and when she kissed me on the cheek, she smelled of Joy perfume and champagne.

There were roughly thirty people in attendance, about fifteen couples, all grey-haired, good-looking, and prosperous: the backbone and pride of the black community – teachers, a physician or two, the women probably members of the Links or the Girlfriends, the kids all in Jack and Jill. Families who attended Episcopal rather than Baptist churches on Sundays and played golf or tennis or bid whist on Saturdays at clubs *outside* of Newark. I could feel people's eyes on me as I entered the room, and knew that we were being viewed as a couple. I was Ben Lennox's date at a gathering of old friends, and they

158

were sizing me up. Was I right for him? Did I fit in? Who was I and where did I come from? I was uncomfortable with this turn into couplehood, but Ben, sensing my discomfort, smiled and squeezed my hand, which had begun to sweat.

The living room was as sterile as I remembered it, and the guests who sat stiffly on the long leather couch balanced their drinks and plates of food carefully on their knees rather than spot the glass coffee table. The dining room was set up as a buffet, laid out with turkey, ham, and salads that were calling my name. I spotted Gus, glass in hand, watching me from the other side of the room. His eyes left me for a moment and settled on his wife, and they exchanged a glance I couldn't interpret. As Gus made his way toward us from across the room, Ben's hand tightened in mine.

'Glad you could finally make it over here,' Gus said, his lips smiling, his eyes empty of expression.

'I wouldn't miss Mattie's birthday, you know that, Gus.' Ben's voice was controlled, and I sensed that something unpleasant had passed between them. I wondered if I had anything to do with it.

'Is Lena here?' Ben asked, his tone demanding more than just the answer to the question.

'No,' Gus said sharply, discouraging any more about her; he turned to me. 'Well, Tamara Hayle, welcome to my home – under more pleasant circumstances. No lies tonight, okay?'

'No lies,' I said lightly, with a good-natured grin, treating it like a joke. But I knew he was serious as hell, and I was embarrassed for a moment, wondering if I should bring up the news about the capture of Shawn Raymond's killer. Then I realized that any mention of Shawn Raymond, be it good or bad, would be about as welcome in this setting as somebody peeing in church.

After about fifteen minutes of meaningless chatter with people I didn't know, I successfully wove my way to the well-laid-out buffet, shamelessly helping myself to turkey, devilled eggs, and potato salad. I've never been one of those women who eat less when they're on a date; it only seems to whet my appetite. Music coming from another room caught my attention, and plate in hand, I headed toward it.

Gina sat at the piano playing chords; her eyes had a faraway look. She wore a white dress, a gauzy number that was too fancy for home and gave her a strange, otherworldly look, like she'd just stepped off the set of *Touched by an Angel.* Her hair was piled high on top of her head in a chignon that was at once little-girlish and bizarre, and her face was pale. She looked so frail and disconnected I wondered if she was on the verge of a nervous breakdown. I remembered what Claudia had said about her addiction to Shawn and what Lena had told me about the drugs, and decided that she was still recovering – from drugs, from Shawn. Baby Gus sat in a baby seat next to the piano, sucking on a pacifier and gazing into space the way babies tend to do.

I clearly understood now why Gus and Mattie had taken Gina in. I said her name softly, afraid of startling her, and she looked up with a smile at once wistful and filled with despair. I saw her now for the victim she had become. I knew about her public humiliation, but what of the times Shawn Raymond had shamed her privately, in ways that she could or would never tell? She was in her own world now as she played, her fingers lightly tripping over the keys. She had obviously been a musician with promise, but was now a shell of what she might have become. The life her parents had dreamed for her had come to shit.

'How are you doing tonight, Gina?' She glanced up once

again, her eyes vacant. 'You are a beautiful and talented woman with so much to offer if you can just make it through this bad time.' I spewed clichés. embarrassed because I could think of nothing meaningful to say. I knew what the real deal was: she was a walking target for another Shawn Raymond who would kill her spirit and claim her self-respect for his own sick amusement.

Gus walked into the room and stood beside her, ignoring my presence, his eyes focused on his daughter as she played. His lips quivered as he watched her, and he closed his eyes as if in prayer, laying his hand very gently on her shoulder. She stopped playing for a moment, dropping her head on his hand, letting it rest as if she was tired. Neither of them spoke or moved. Whatever else I knew about Gus Lennox – about his meanness, his need to dominate, his cruelty – I was sure at this moment that he loved his daughter in his own strange way with everything he had to give.

I left to join the others in the dining room, where Mattie was preparing to cut her cake, and soon Gus and Gina joined the rest of the group, Gus moving to the front of the room, Gina holding her baby to her breast and sitting away from everybody else. I also noticed Zeke, who had managed to edge himself against a far wall, roaming the room with his eyes, his glance lingering on each of the guests as if he were searching them for some weakness or secret. *What had he been like as a young man?* I wondered. *Had he really been the killer and thief Gina had said he was?* His eyes caught mine, and I looked away quickly.

'A bottle of Moët for your thoughts?' Ben joked. His breath tickling my ear sent a thrill through me. I smiled what I hoped was a mysterious, seductive smile.

* * *

The cake was cut and eaten, the champagne drunk, and most of the guests gone home, when Ben and I finally sat down in the kitchen with Gus and Mattie. The kitchen was a large one, comfortable, homey, and obviously designed for somebody who liked to cook. The appliances, all stainless steel and spotless, looked new, or maybe it was just Mattie's expertise with a cleaning rag, a skill for which I had developed a keen appreciation. Sheer curtains hung at each window and six wooden chairs encircled the long kitchen table.

Too easily, I slipped into the role of drudge I'd been playing for the last couple of weeks and helped Mattie do the last of the cleaning, while Ben and Gus, in annoying male fashion, sipped bourbon and watched us work. I'd caught Gus staring at me several times during the evening, as if trying to understand something about me. I'd smiled pleasantly each time, but he hadn't returned my smile. Although I didn't think Mattie and I could ever become friends – swapping confidences, hanging out at the mall – washing dishes together does bring its own bond and I liked her more than I had before. We chatted quietly, oblivious of Ben and Gus as they finished off leftover corn chips and salsa. Zeke had found his way into the kitchen, and sat near his brothers. I noticed for the first time just how much the three resembled each other, even their voices had the same timbre, nearly the same pitch. They were as tied by blood and history as I was tied to Johnny.

Suddenly Gus stood up, wobbling slightly and hoisting his glass of bourbon as if he was going to make a toast. Ben shook his head in disgust and clapped his brother on the back, urging him to sit back down, and tossed me an amused smile, his eyes saying he hoped I felt comfortable enough now to join in this family giddiness. I sensed that whatever differences had been between them at the beginning of the evening had been resolved.

I grinned back, noticing that even Zeke, as if caught in some sweet memory from their past, was smiling.

'To my brothers,' Gus said as he drunkenly threw his arms around Ben and coaxed Zeke to stand close to him. Ben glanced at me and rolled his eyes, but he couldn't hide the tenderness he felt for his brothers. 'And to my wife Mattie on her birthday. And to Newark, my city,' Gus added, and he and Ben clicked glasses noisily.

'And to new old friends,' Ben added, with a nod toward me. 'But to Newark, Gus?'

'It is coming back,' Gus said, stumbling backward slightly, and catching himself. 'This city is coming back. That Arts Centre they finished, all those new houses over there where those projects used to be. Pretty soon you'll be able to see Herman and the Bluenotes and Patti and the Bluebells without going to the Apollo.'

'It was Melvin and the Bluenotes and the only way that you will hear Melvin sing again is if you join him in heaven – the brother passed away. And for that matter, Patti ain't sung with Nona and Sarah since I was in high school. Get out the past, brother, or get it right!' joked Ben. Mattie, her eyes gleaming, chuckled at her husband.

'No, no, man. You can't forget the past, man,' Gus argued as he poured himself another drink. 'The past will always set you straight. The past is what makes the future. There ain't no future without the past.' He looked pensive for a moment as he rocked back on his feet, and suddenly he glanced at me, as if I should understand how our pasts were tied.

'Let's not talk about the past,' said Mattie, her voice wary and flat, the tilt of her head sending a warning. Gus chose to ignore it.

'Sometimes I feel like that's all I got,' Gus whined. He was pathetically drunk, more clownish than anything else.

'My brother was a hero cop,' Ben said, feeling the need to explain. 'But I guess you've heard that.'

'Mattie, show her the book,' Gus said.

'She doesn't want to see the book,' Mattie said.

'Show her the damn book,' Gus ordered. His voice had a rusty edge as he settled back into his chair. Mattie looked helpless, almost frightened.

'She doesn't want to see the book.' Her voice shook. Ben came to her rescue.

'We all know you were a hero cop, Gus. Now go to bed,' he said softly but firmly, as if he were talking to a sleepy, spoiled child.

'Show her the goddamn book,' Gus said, his voice now louder and more threatening. I wondered why it was so important that I – obviously the 'her' he was referring to – had to see what was in his book, what it was he wanted to impress me with.

'Go to bed, Gus, you're stinking drunk,' Ben said.

'What's in the book?' I asked.

'Newspaper articles about him and the old days. About the—' Mattie's voice broke as she choked on the word. Gus slammed his glass on the table dramatically, like a judge slams down a gavel.

'Let me say something.'

'Go to bed, Gus,' Ben said.

'I just want to make a statement.'

'A statement?' Ben asked incredulously. 'What kind of a statement could you possibly need to make at one-thirty in the morning?'

'There is a strain of losers in this damn city that's got to be wiped out like vermin,' Gus said. 'Needs to be allowed to just wither and die before they bring the rest of us down there with them. The white boys got it right! We need to let a generation go to hell, fuck 'em, just let 'em go. You know what I'm talking about.' Ben stared at his brother in stunned disbelief.

'Shut the hell up and go to bed, Gus. That liquor is saying things you don't want it to be saying.'

'One more toast?' Gus's voice was sly as he glanced toward Zeke, whose dark look had returned.

Mattie looked uneasy, Ben obviously distressed.

'One more goddamn toast!' Gus said again. 'One more?'

Ben threw me a flustered glance and picked up his glass, which was mostly melted ice. 'Man, when did it get so bad that you couldn't hold your liquor?' He watched helplessly as his brother topped his glass with bourbon.

'To the Prince Street Gang. And all the filth they brought into this city and all the filth I flushed out,' Gus toasted reverently, lifting his glass dramatically with a side glance at Zeke, whose face was suddenly contorted in rage. 'To the Prince Street Gang!'

The room was as silent as if a curse had been shouted, and then Zeke grabbed the bottle of bourbon, broke it in half, and lunged to slash his brother's throat.

'Why you want to take it there, man? Why the fuck you want to take it there?' Mattie moaned in horror, and Ben pushed her to the side as he jumped between his brothers, separating them with his body, knocking the bottle out of Zeke's hand, and pushing Gus out of his way. Zeke's fist pounded down on Gus's face and chest. 'Goddamn you, man. Goddamn you.'

'Enough, damn it! That's enough! That's it,' Ben yelled as Gus collapsed on to the table and Zeke, panting and cursing, moved away.

I, standing completely still, didn't realize until I started breathing again that I had stopped.

'Come on, baby, we're out of here as soon as I help Mattie put this fool to bed. These two assholes don't know how to behave,' Ben muttered, trembling with anger.

'I'm sorry,' Mattie kept repeating as she wept, her hands covering her face. Ben grabbed Gus roughly by the shoulders and waist and pulled and shoved him out of the kitchen. Mattie, crying, walked behind him. I turned back to the spotless sink, scrubbing it in a frenzy. Feeling Zeke's eyes on me, I turned to face him.

'Leave me alone,' I said. 'I know who you are and why they call you Chee-chee.' I threw it out in tough-girl fashion because I don't like feeling afraid of a man, and that was how I felt. But the way his eyes narrowed and his neck and fist stiffened made me wish I'd kept my mouth shut.

'You don't know what you're talking about, you filthy, stupid little bitch,' he said. 'You. You. See what you done brought in here. See it!' He turned and left the room then, bumping against the table and knocking one of the chairs on its side. I picked up the chair and collapsed into it after the doors had swung closed, my heart beating fast as I listened for Ben. But all I could hear was the sound of Gina playing 'Amazing Grace' on the piano in the other room.

Ben stared without blinking at the empty road ahead of us as he drove me home about fifteen minutes later. 'I'm sorry about that, Tamara, about what happened. I don't know where all that came from with Zeke. This is the first time they've really talked about any of it in front of me. That whole mess with the Prince Street Gang went down when I was a kid.'

'So he busted that gang up by going undercover?' I was still shaking. I held my hands together in my lap so Ben couldn't see me trembling.

'It was his one big moment of glory, infiltrating that gang like he did, turning them in. First time he killed a man, though, and I know that messed with him big-time, killing a man like that. It was real action-movie stuff.'

'So Zeke was a member of this Prince Street Gang.' I was guessing about Zeke's connection from what he'd said tonight, from the little I knew about his past. 'Do you think maybe that was how Gus got into it so easily, because of Zeke? Gangs are like family. They only let somebody in if somebody vouches for him.'

A shadow passed over Ben's face. 'Yeah, that's how Gus got in. But he didn't betray anyone,' he added defensively, as if he sensed that was what I thought. 'Thieves have no honor to betray.'

'How about brothers?' He didn't say anything to that, just kept his eyes glued to that road.

Jamal was watching videos on BET, sneakers off, munching popcorn when I came into the house. He was waiting up, he said, because he wanted to ask me about spending Friday night with one of his basketball teammates, and since the friend lived near Annie, he could scoot over the next morning and clean up her garage like I'd promised he would. I was distracted as he spoke, my mind still on Ben and the scene I'd just left.

'I'm also driving the Blue Demon, by the way,' he threw out to see if I was really listening to him, which I wasn't. 'Just testing you, Ma. To see if you heard me,' he said quickly when I glanced up. 'What's wrong?'

'Nothing.'

'Where did you go?'

'Birthday party.'

'Have a good time?'

'More or less.'

'Did you go with that guy who's been calling?'

'Ben Lennox? Yes.'

'Do you like him?'

'He seems like a good man,' I said casually, taking off my coat and turning my back so he couldn't read anything on my face. 'He doesn't lie to me, tells me his secrets, takes me to eat at nice places, that kind of stuff.'

'Word? I like that,' Jamal said thoughtfully, like somebody's parent, and we both laughed. 'So when can I check him out?' I settled down on the couch next to him and gave the top of his head a rub, like I've done since he was a little boy.

'Soon,' I said, surprised myself by how quickly I answered.

Ten

'You better tell your girl Annie to get that door fixed sometime before the Second Coming. It's been broke more than a week,' Wyvetta Green said as I came into the building that Friday morning. She was standing at the door of the Biscuit with a cup of coffee in her hand and a take-no-shit scowl on her face. Her hair, light brown for the last few weeks (she had not given up on that Jada Pinkett mess), was now back to its natural colour and plastered sleek and black against her head.

I knew what she was talking about. I'd cursed out the door myself the night before when I had to slam it three times to get the lock to catch. I'd meant to call Annie about it when I got home, but Ben had called after dinner and we'd talked until midnight about nothing in particular and I'd gone to sleep with him on my mind and that broken door the farthest thing from my thoughts. I bent over now to examine it, searching for any hint that it had been tampered with, but it looked like old age and poor maintenance had simply taken their toll.

'I'll give Annie a call when I get upstairs, and mention it to her,' I said in a sweet, agreeable voice. You don't want to tangle with Wyvetta Green when she's got a 'tude problem, as Karen would put it.

'Don't just mention it, *tell* the woman to do something about it. You never know who the hell is going to walk in here.'

169

Wyvetta banged her coffee cup on the table and slammed a drawer shut. 'And you can tell Miss Annie B. Landlord that she won't get her rent this month if she don't have that door fixed by the time it's due. All we need is for somebody to come strolling in here toting a gun.'

I reared up and checked Wyvetta out, wondering what had gotten into her. I can count the number of times that she's snapped at me first thing in the morning. Wyvetta is one of the proudest, friendliest women I know, and she does not like to lose her temper over foolishness. Obviously something had pissed the sister off.

'"Toting a gun", Wyvetta?' I stuffed the bills I'd just gotten out of the mailbox we share into my bag, handed her the ones that belonged to her, and stepped into the Biscuit, settling down in one of her chairs.

'Just tell her to fix it, that's all.' Wyvetta began to fold towels in neat white triangles, mechanically placing them on the table in front of her. It was still too early for clients, and I could hear Lucy in the back of the shop washing out her tools and trying to sing like Mary J. Blige. I watched Wyvetta folding the towels in the mirror in front of us, her lips pursed in a tight line, her nimble fingers snapping them into shape. When she caught me studying her, she plopped down in the chair next to me sighing heavily. 'Girl, I'm sorry. My nerves are b-a-d *bad* this morning. I better get myself together before I tackle them heads. Maybe I should take a nip of that Johnny Walker Red that Earl keeps stashed in the back.'

'You better take a nip of something.' Wyvetta stood up like she was looking for something to do, and then sat back down.

'Things have gotten so bad in this damn city you can't hardly breathe.'

'Things have *been* bad, Wyvetta.'

170

'Not as bad as this. You didn't hear about it on the radio? That's all that's been on it. If they can shoot somebody for nothing, just trying to go into their house, no telling what they'll do they think you got a little money on you. Lucy, bring in that paper so we can see if there's something in it.'

'What happened?'

'Some lady coming in her house last night, into her own house, got out her car walking to her door, nothing on her mind except where she'd been and *bam*! Before she could think two good thoughts, before she could even kiss her sweet ass goodbye, somebody killed her. Shot her dead! Ain't even safe to go in your own house no more. Lucy, did you find that paper yet?'

Lucy, studying the *Star-Ledger*, came in from the back, sank into the chair next to Wyvetta, and glanced up at me, her eyes wide with disbelief.

'That's why I'm so mad about that damn door,' said Wyvetta, her voice lowered confidentially. 'I could do some crazy woman's hair and next thing I know, she'll be in here with an AK-47 talking about I ruined her looks and blow us all away! Ain't nowhere safe these days.'

'But who would want to kill her?' Lucy said to herself.

'It could have been a hit,' I said, offering a detached, professional opinion on something I knew nothing about. 'Probably somebody she knew. It might have been about drugs or revenge. It could have a jealous boyfriend, an abusive husband, or a botched robbery. Wyvetta, I'll call Annie as soon as I get upstairs,' I said, reaching to take the newspaper from Lucy as I stood up to leave.

'Oh, Miss Hayle, I'm so sorry,' Lucy said. The odd, bewildered look in the girl's eyes made my heart quicken.

'Lucy, what's wrong with you?' Wyvetta asked impatiently,

curious about that strange look too.

'It was Miss Hayle's friend.' Lucy avoided my eyes, focusing on Wyvetta instead as she folded the paper in front of her in four sections like a fan and handed it to me. 'It was Gina, Miss Hayle. Gina Lennox who had that pretty little baby you were talking about a few weeks ago. Gina Lennox was the one who got shot last night.'

The Lennox block was eerily quiet when I drove up to it about fifteen minutes later. The shades were pulled down at nearly every house, as if to shut out the possibility of violence striking again. Although the day was bright with morning sun, and the air had a bracing crispness to it, the street was deserted. No cars were parked, no children rode tricycles on the sidewalk, no dogs yelped for attention. Signs of the tragedy still lingered ominously. Cigarette and candy wrappers left by the cops were scattered on the sidewalk and street. Trash cans had been overturned; their soiled contents spilled out into the yards. Paths had been trampled in the neat lawns, the well-kept street violated.

Yellow tape was sloppily draped around the area where Gina had been murdered. Ten feet on the sidewalk and part of the porch and stairs were roped off. Traces of her blood had seeped into the porch and the surrounding areas. I closed my eyes, bracing myself against the nausea that swept me. Someone had placed a bedraggled bouquet of white and pink carnations on the sidewalk near a pile of dead leaves about two feet away from the roped-off area. I picked up the flowers and smelled them, feeling the moist, soft petals against my nose, trying to remember Gina as I had last seen her, when she had been lost in her music, her eyes filled with despair.

My sister would be better off dead.

They were words angrily and thoughtlessly uttered that I knew would haunt Lena Lennox and be regretted for the rest of her life. Gina was as dead as Shawn Raymond now; it was as if he had reached up from his grave and pulled her down to that level too. It had been months since his death, yet only weeks since I had begun asking questions, kicking up dust, giving the dead no peace at all. I thought again about my last talk with Gina.

I told you all I can. All I will.

All she ever could. All she ever would.

Were these killings just random coincidence? I didn't think so. Osborne's suspect was only as strong as the confessions 'squeezed' out of him, and a squeezed confession has about as much juice as a squeezed orange. I edged the carnations under the yellow rope, pushing them as far as I could toward the spot where Gina had died, saying a prayer for her. Ben Lennox touched my arm, startling me.

'I saw you when you drove up. Thank you for coming.' He had come outside without a coat, and his thin blue sweater and jeans offered little protection against the chill. His ashen face and swollen, red eyes told me that he had probably spent the night crying. I followed him to the backyard, and we entered the Lennox house through the back door.

The kitchen counters were already piled high with food dropped off by caring neighbours and friends. Covered dishes, a casserole or two, and several pies draped in aluminium foil were crowded together on the counter. Plates and glasses were in the sink, and pots and pans, obviously left from breakfast, were still on the stove. Two nights ago I'd watched Ben Lennox fight his brothers around this table, but that time seemed long ago. In another part of the house, I could hear Gina's baby crying, his screams piercing the quiet house. I'd forgotten about baby Gus, and what Gina's murder would do to his young life. My eyes watered at the thought of it.

'He's been screaming on and off like that all night,' Ben said quietly. 'It's like he knows something terrible has happened. How do you explain to a baby that his mother is dead, that he will never see her again?' We sat stiffly, our bodies barely touching, listening to the baby wail, hoping he would stop his anguished cries. I could hear someone pacing back and forth in the living room, and someone talking in a low, deep voice. I took Ben's cool, moist hand in mine. His voice cracked as he told his tale.

'She was coming in around ten. She came out the car. Nobody was on the street. Somebody must have confronted her, maybe waiting for her behind that big oak out there, the one that separates our house from Joe Simpson's. Damn, I thought so many times that we should have pruned that tree, cut those damn bushes down. If we had, maybe he couldn't have—'

'There was nothing you could have done.'

He shook his head as if he didn't believe me. 'Mattie heard something, sounded like a firecracker. It was loud like that, sudden like that, and she thought it was some kids, playing with something they shouldn't be, you know how kids do. Gus ran out. He'd heard it too, but he knew what it was. Gina was dead. She was gone before he even got to her.'

'How are they doing, Mattie and Gus?'

He shook his head again, dejectedly, without answering.

'How long were the police here?'

'Most of last night. This morning. They left right before you got here. Them and the papers.'

'Do they have any idea why she was killed?'

'No.'

'How many shots were fired?' Ben cringed, and I

174

immediately regretted the insensitivity that comes from the cop part of me that always wants the facts. The newspaper hadn't mentioned the number of shots.

'One. Through the heart.'

Like Shawn Raymond.

He stood up and went to the sink, got down a glass from the cabinet and turned on the faucet. His hands were trembling. I could see the water shaking as it filled his glass. The baby had finally stopped crying and the house was quiet again, but it was an uncomfortable silence, one filled with sorrow. I began putting the covered food in the refrigerator, more for something to do than anything else. The only sounds were the refrigerator door as I opened and closed it and the scrape of the dishes against the shelves. I was conscious of Ben's breathing, how shallow and rapid it had become, as if he were out of breath. He sat back down and closed his eyes.

Suddenly there were footsteps on the back walk. I listened as they approached, the hard, fast click of the heels walking and then running up the stairs. Lena Lennox, her face veiled in grief, her eyes swollen from crying, burst through the back door, her bright raincoat open and flying around her like scarlet wings. Ben stood up, opening his mouth as if to speak, but she held up both hands silencing him and shook her head, as if to tell him she didn't want to hear what he had to say.

'Don't try to stop me,' she warned as he moved toward her, grabbing her hand and pulling her toward him. She snatched it away, making her way through the swinging kitchen doors into the living room, and the silence was broken by her shrieking voice.

'Goddamn you! You son of a bitch! Look what you've done, you son of a bitch!' I heard a man scream out in rage and then again in anguish. There was the tinkle of something shattering, and then the muffled, blunt sound of flesh hitting flesh. Ben and I dashed into the living room, both of us afraid of what we would find.

They were all here now. All the Lennox family. The crystal knick-knacks from the glass coffee table lay in a smattering of sparkling shards on the spotless white rug. Ben stood by me near the kitchen door, his eyes filled with dread. Lena lay on the floor, the fading imprint of a hand red on her face. Gus stood above her, his hand still raised, his mouth twisted in anger, tears spilling from his eyes. Zeke sat on the couch, rocking back and forth, his arms flung around his body as if trying to calm himself or put himself to sleep. Mattie lay on the couch next to him, her fists balled up in her mouth. The baby nestled close to her breast, his eyes open, staring at nothing.

'You reap what you sow. You reap what you sow. You reap what you sow. You reap what you sow.' Lena repeated the words in a hypnotic, hysterical chant. The baby began to whimper, adding his own anguish to the sorrowful scene. Zeke's eyes caught mine, narrowing with malice.

'Get the fuck out of here,' he said to me from his spot on the couch. 'You know what I told you yesterday, get the fuck away from us.'

'Can you leave us now?' Ben glanced back at me, pleading, his eyes begging me to listen, his voice trembling. 'Please, Tamara, please leave us now!'

I returned to the kitchen, and sat down at the table. But I could still hear them, whispering, crying, begging to each other in voices nearly indistinguishable.

They had reaped Gina's death. How had they sown it?

I unloaded the dishwasher, mechanically taking out the clean dishes and loading it up again with dirty ones. I filled the sink with hot water and liquid Joy, dumped all the dirty pots into it, let them soak for a moment or two, finding the lemon smell of the dishwashing liquid and the warmth of the water soothing as I scrubbed and rinsed them. The house was silent now; even the baby had stopped crying. I glanced around the kitchen looking for something else to do, wondering about this family and the secrets that they kept.

'Don't go yet,' Ben said, entering the kitchen as I was putting on my coat. He pulled me toward him, holding me for a moment, not a sexual embrace but one of simple comfort. 'Can I come with you?'

'Come with me?' I stuttered out the words, not sure for a moment what he meant.

'Yes.' He looked agitated, almost frightened. 'Wherever you're going. I just have to be with you for a while.'

'But Ben—'

'Please, Tamara. I can't be alone now. Not now. I can't stay here.'

'Where do you want to go?' His face was blank, completely empty.

'Anywhere but here. Back to your place maybe? Please.'

He followed me out of the house, without his coat, like a kid who needs to be taken care of, and that was the way he looked as he leaned back in the passenger seat of my car, like a broken, scared little boy. His head fell limply against his window, and his shoulders slumped. I gave him a sideways glance as I waited for the Jetta to cough itself awake. He seemed so different now, so changed from our first date in the Pinnacle. He had been so confident and self-assured that night – talking, flirting, teasing – a strong, fine brother with everything working for him, everything together. He closed his eyes; his eyelashes were longer than I remembered them. I could see the gentle baby brother in his face, the little boy who had battled for his identity in the tight, brutal space left by his older brothers.

'How are you feeling, Ben?'

'More tired than I've ever been in my life.'

'Is there anywhere in particular you want to go?'

'I just want to ride.'

I popped in an Abby Lincoln tape, *A Turtle's Dream*, that I'd gotten from Jake and drove, stopping first by my office to return some calls and pick up some work to do over the weekend. I left him sleeping in my car as I dashed into the Pathmark to pick up a few things and then made it to the dry cleaner's. It was nearly five by the time I pulled into my driveway, glad that I'd given Jamal permission to spend the night away from home, and that it was dark enough to keep my nosy neighbors out of my business.

We sat down at the kitchen table, and I made us some sandwiches. After we finished eating, I found half a bottle of Courvoisier I'd forgotten I had and two brandy snifters, and poured us each a glass.

'Thank you,' he said.

'For what?'

'For not leaving me by myself in that house.' I wanted to ask him about that house, but sensed that it was not yet the time.

'Where's your son?'

'Out. For the night.'

He took a sip of brandy. 'That's probably a good thing.'

'Yeah,' I agreed. It probably was. 'Why don't you tell me what's bothering you, Ben?'

'Nothing.'

'It's something to do with Gina's and Shawn's deaths, isn't it?' I ignored his quick answer.

'It's nothing. Why don't you believe me?'

I told you all I can, all I will.

178

'Did I tell you that the cops think they've caught the man who shot Raymond?' He looked startled for a moment, and fear or something close to it flickered in his eyes.

'How am I supposed to react to that?' he said, which surprised me.

'You tell me.'

'Great! Is that what you want me to say? I told you that first night we went out how I felt about the son of a bitch.' He stood up and walked into the living room, glancing at the photos of my family on the bookshelf, and the framed prints I have on my wall, finally settling down on my couch as I joined him. 'As long as I've known you I've never been in your house. Maybe that once, before the prom when I came by to get you, do you remember that?' he said more gently. I did remember it, and the memory made me smile.

'You grew up here, in this house?'

'Here and Newark. The Hayes Homes when I was a kid.'

He chuckled, like he was remembering something funny. 'Newark. It's like family, your mama or your daddy, isn't it? You can talk about it bad, but don't let anybody else do it. I never had the same connection to the city that Gus has. The same sense of ownership, the same need to protect it.'

'Why do you think that is?'

He leaned back, took another sip of brandy. 'Going away like I did when I was a kid, first out of state to that prep school they sent me to, then away to college, then grad school . . . I never really lived in Newark after that. Even now when I'm here, I'm always glad to go back home at night. I'm not of the city anymore. My only connection is my brothers.'

'And what is that connection?'

'More than I want to talk about.' He sipped at his brandy again.

179

'Why did they send you away when you were so young?' I asked, remembering how sudden it had seemed when he left, sensing how uncomfortable any mention of his family made him, wanting to give him the benefit of the doubt.

Ben shrugged. 'Now when I think about it, I know it must have been because of whatever went down between them,' he said, bringing the conversation back to his brothers.

'There is so much anger between them. Killing rage,' I said, thinking with a shudder of how eagerly Zeke had gone for Gus's throat. 'How do they stand it, living together like that?'

'For one thing, Zeke has nowhere else to go. And that anger is not there most of the time.'

'Something stirred it up again.'

'Yeah.' He dropped his head. 'Something did.'

'And what was that something, Ben?' I tried probing again. He looked at me strangely.

'I can't, Tamara.'

'You won't.'

'No, I won't.'

'Why won't you?'

'Tamara, please don't put me through this now. Later maybe, but not tonight, please.' There was such anguish in his voice and on his face I let it lay, knowing that at some point I'd have to come back to it. As if in gratitude, he took my hand, brought it to his lips, kissing each of my fingers. I pulled away, took another sip of brandy, knowing what he was doing and not being fooled. We sat there on the couch awhile longer. I put some CDs on – Cassandra Wilson, Erykah Badu, and finally some early Miles that reminded me of my father.

'I still remember that first time,' he said.

'Last time,' I corrected him.

'Not the last time.' He kissed me once and then quickly again.

180

I liked the way his mouth felt, and the way his tongue separated my lips, and I knew at that moment that we would make love.

My decision was not some quick, hot sudden loss of control and better judgement. There is only one man on earth who has that effect on me. My desire for Ben, while ardent, was safer, saner. Truth be told, I knew I would sleep with Ben Lennox that first night at the Pinnacle, when we'd stayed together longer than I'd planned, and his kiss, though fleeting, had brought back the hot sexual rush of that time we'd made love. I was sure of it after our first late-night conversation, when I'd fallen asleep with him on my mind, imagining how his body would feel next to mine. We had a shared remembrance, a sensual, carnal memory of that night years ago, and I knew tonight that I wanted to feel that way with him again.

My bedroom was cold when we entered, cooler than it usually is, or maybe I noticed it more because someone was coming into it with me. We slipped out of our clothing quickly, and I put the condoms I'd picked up at the Pathmark where I could easily reach them. We joked for an instant about how things had changed between consenting adults when it came to sex, and I found myself chuckling and enjoying his sense of humour as I always did, and I liked that feeling too. We rushed under the down comforter, drawing together for warmth and the feel of our bodies together. The sheets smelled faintly of the jojoba oil lotion I'd been using and blended with the lemon scent of his cologne. I stretched my body the full length of his, feeling his strength and warmth against me, and I was swept by a quick, sweet pull of desire, and my need to feel him inside me.

My body and senses remember each man who has ever touched me. As Ben's fingers lightly stroked me, I remembered for a moment the last man I'd slept with – the passion and thrill of it all. The memory of his touch and the feel of his lips

181

blending with those of Ben added to my excitement. But I brought myself back to Ben, to *his* touch and smell, and the feel of *his* lips against my skin and his embrace, and of what we meant to each other once, what we meant now, again. There was a warm familiarity as he caressed my neck, my breasts with his lips and his tongue. He had been a good lover – a thoughtful, generous one. I had liked that about him the first time, and that had not changed. When finally he came into me, and I lost myself in him, I was happy that we had finally found each other again.

When he was asleep, I drew away from him, studying his face and the muscular arm that was flung over the space where my body had been. I wondered for a moment if I had made a mistake, and if that secret he wouldn't tell would make me regret tonight. But as I lay back down beside him, and he reached for me, grazing my breasts with his fingers, I made myself believe that it wouldn't. We had brought each other joy on a day filled with sorrow. Maybe that was enough to be thankful for.

Eleven

The next morning the phone rang five times before I scrambled out of bed to answer it. It was Jamal, calling to tell me that his friend's father had tickets to a Knicks game that night and had invited him to come along. He wanted me to drop off a pair of clean jeans and a sweater at Annie's so he could pick it up later in the morning when he stopped by to clean up her garage. A grin broke out on my face. I was eager to spend more time with Ben and not quite ready to hop back into the motherhood thing, so Jamal's plans fit smoothly into mine. But I agreed too quickly. I could hear his antenna wind up.

'So, uh, Ma, you just getting up?'

'It's seven o'clock in the morning.'

'Yeah. So what'd you do last night?'

'Nothing.'

'So, what you doing now?'

'Talking to you.'

'So what you doing tonight?'

'I haven't made plans yet.' I wondered what he was fishing for.

'So, uh, you going to go out with that Ben Lennox dude again?'

'That's a possibility. I'll drop off your things, and see you later on tonight, okay?' I hung up quickly, cutting off the possibility of his reeling in a catch. Obviously it was time for me to introduce him to Ben, who was still asleep beside me. I nudged him gently to see if he would awaken easily, but he didn't move. He slept very hard, his breathing deep, his hands clenched into fists. I showered, dressed, and found some clean clothes for Jamal mixed up with the dirty ones on the floor in his messy room. Then I went downstairs to the kitchen, brewed a pot of coffee, and drank a cup while I scribbled a note telling Ben I'd be back in an hour and we'd have breakfast together. I was in a remarkably good mood as I backed out of my driveway and headed to Annie's. It was Saturday, the sun was shining, and sex never fails to lift my spirits. But even as I tried to keep my mind on Ben Lennox, the words that Lena had spoken yesterday, the ones about reaping what was sown, kept popping back. I was making too much of the whole damn thing, I finally decided.

It's amazing what your mind will rationalise if you let it, and I let mine have its way with me that morning. What I had witnessed, I told myself, had been nothing more than a family's grief. Lena had reaped what she'd sown when she introduced Shawn Raymond to her sister, and she had reaped the pain she had sown with her family. When Gus Lennox slapped his daughter's face, he was probably just slapping the girl out of her hysterics. Zeke's words, as disgusting and profane as they were, could have been his way of protecting a privacy that he felt I had violated. After all, my first interaction with the Lennoxes had been on behalf of Shawn Raymond, and although it was clear to me now who the man had become, I had been his advocate. It was natural for them to distrust me.

I made myself recall the tenderness with which Ben and I had made love the night before. Shawn Raymond was dead. Gina Lennox was dead. Ben's reaction to the news of the capture of Shawn's killer had seemed a bit strange, but why shouldn't it? He didn't give a damn about Shawn Raymond, one way or the other. When I thought about it, his reaction was just about right. Ben had told me that he had nothing to hide. Why couldn't I just take him at his word? I'd just spent the night with the man, hadn't I? I pulled into Annie's driveway determined to forget any misgivings, and I did a good job. I rang her back doorbell with Ben Lennox and our night together on my mind. Annie read my face like a lottery ticket.

'Well, *who* has got you glowing like this?' she asked as she scrutinised me. 'And it's not even noon yet! What are you doing up so early on a Saturday morning? Come on in here, girl, and tell me where you spent Friday night.'

'This cold weather has got me glowing like this, and I spent last night at home in my bed,' I added truthfully, with a dignified nod that I hoped would put an end to her speculation. No such luck. 'So did you talk to Jamal?' I asked as I handed her the bag with his clothes in it.

'You mean to say Jamal is not at home?' She was doubly suspicious now.

'No, he spent the night with one of the guys on his team. He did say he'd be over here to help you this morning with that garage, though. I'm dropping these things off for him. He's going to a Knicks game tonight, and he's going to change over here.'

'If cold air put that much shine in your eyes, you wouldn't have all these sisters buying minks. You can't fool me.'

'Annie, get your cheap, vicarious little thrills from somebody else's sex life,' I said as I slid down into one of her chairs. The kitchen smelled like cinnamon and apples, and my stomach started to rumble with hunger.

'So you ain't talking yet?'

185

'There's nothing to talk about, Annie – nothing that's your business anyway.'

'Take off your coat and stay awhile. Have you had breakfast? I just fried some apples if you want some. Biscuits are in the oven.'

'No, thanks. I'm going to have to be getting back home, I—'

'Hold on, baby. I have never in my life known Tamara Hayle to turn down a plate of fried apples and biscuits. Jamal's not at home. You come in here beaming like you're in love. You must think I just fell off a turnip truck – I know something's up when I see it. So he's nice, huh? And don't bother with his name. I'll get that from Jamal later on.'

'What is it with you married people, that you always think a single person's love life is open for discussion?'

She waved me away, as if dismissing me. 'Oh, come on and sit on down here and have some of these apples. I made too many, and William's still sleep. I need the company. They'll look better on your hips than on mine.'

'No, I'd better get back—'

'In time to grab another quickie?'

'Okay! You win!' I said with mild but amused irritation.

'So who is this Mr Nameless?'

'Mr Nameless.'

'Is it that fine, fine, *fine* Jamaican brother who—'

'No, Annie, it's not him.' I cut off her reminiscences about my personal past as she brought me a saucerful of fried apples. Tempted beyond resistance, I took a healthy forkful.

'Stick around. Biscuits will be out in a minute,' she said, pouring herself a cup of coffee. I had another forkful, and picked up a pile of photos that lay near the sugar bowl.

'They're from that trip you've been too busy to hear about,' Annie scolded as I shuffled through them. They were the kind of pictures you'd expect from a cruise: elaborate food displays, men in scant bikinis, glassy-eyed women holding drinks decorated with tropical fruits. As I held each one up, Annie enthusiastically identified it.

'Midnight buffet,' she explained about a large glossy picture of a seafood spread featuring lobster tails and mounds of shrimp. 'Girl, I ate so much salmon I almost made myself sick. It was embarrassing. I can't even stand to smell it any more. It's a shame!'

'That was the formal night,' she said as I showed one of her and several of her sorors dressed to the nines in long dresses and shawls. 'William wore that tux I got him last Christmas. Finally got to wear that long orange dress Mama claims is as loud as a church choir.'

'What was the name of your ship?'

'The *Odyssey*. Want some coffee with those apples?'

I stopped shuffling.

'The line is called Odyssey Adventures. Nice ship. Big staterooms. Good casino. I even won a hundred dollars in the quarter slots – put it all back though. William was totally disgusted. I'm telling you, Tamara, you would love it. Even the money isn't too bad if you think about everything you get.'

'So where did the ship stop?' I was curious now.

Annie grinned as she remembered. 'Well, we started off in Aruba, and then to the San Blas Islands in Panama, the Canal, Costa Rica, and oh yeah, Cartagena.' She rolled her eyes. 'How can I forget Cartagena! So why are you so interested in my cruise all of a sudden?' she said as she possessively snatched back the pictures and rifled through them herself, a big smile on her face.

'So what happened in Cartagena?'

She wrinkled her forehead as if recalling an unpleasant

187

memory. 'It wasn't the city. It's one of the prettiest cities I've ever seen. Full of ancient, narrow streets that look like they could lead to all kinds of adventures. Very romantic, old architecture. Despite what you see in travel books, Colombia, Brazil, Peru, all those Central and South American countries are filled with black folks. Those slave ships definitely deposited their cargo there. There were times I got off the boat and thought I was on the corner of Broad and Market.'

'So what happened in Cartagena?' I tried to get her back on track.

'Somebody lifted one of my sorors' passport, Pauline from Dallas. That place is beautiful, but it's like the Wild, Wild West. There's a lot of criminal activity and drug smuggling going on. Pauline didn't find out it was gone until she got ready to disembark in San Juan. Left a bad taste in everybody's mouth.'

'They didn't check your passports in other ports, when you got on and off the ship each time it docked?'

'All you have to show the crew is a special pass with your name and cabin number on it. Luckily Pauline had that in her pocket. As long as you have that pass you're okay. Nobody on the ship is going to hassle you, if you know what I mean. They pretty much know who belongs on the ship and who doesn't, so when you get on or off, they don't do formal head counts or anything like that.'

I stopped sipping my coffee and placed my fork down next to the saucer filled with fried apples. 'So as long as you have that pass, you can get off or back on if you want to, and nobody really knows or has any record of it one way or the other?'

Annie thought about it for a moment. 'Well, I mean somebody is bound to know, like the person you're travelling with. If you missed the boat, I assume somebody would tell the captain, and they'd wait for you or something. If you were by yourself, then I guess your table partners and waiter would know. What's up, Tamara? Are you thinking about a cruise?'

The fried apples had turned mushy and heavy in my mouth. I didn't think I could swallow them. A sense of dread swept me.

'What's wrong, girl?' Annie said with concern. 'You look like you've seen a ghost.'

I had, and his name was Shawn Raymond.

Ben was sitting at the kitchen table when I came in the door. His back was to me, and for a moment I wasn't sure that he knew I had come in. His hand rested on his coffee cup as if he had just picked it up or put it back down, and he nodded his head slightly every now and then as if he were engaged in some silent, disturbing conversation with himself.

How involved with Shawn Raymond's death had he been? I wondered. Where does his guilt begin and end? Who on that cruise had gotten back to Jersey and pulled the trigger that snuffed out that man's life? Had it been Gus, who had the biggest motive of all? Ben doing it as a brotherly favour? Even Mattie was suspect. The motive had always been there, and I should have known that a killer will always find a way. And his death had brought the other, the one that had led him to my bed last night.

I stood and watched him for another moment or two and then settled down in the chair across from him, and we stared at each other for a while without speaking. I felt sad, then embarrassed that I had been taken in by him, and then angrier than I like to be at anybody, and he must have seen it on my face, because he dropped his head in shame. Maybe he could read my thoughts; I've never been much good at hiding my feelings. Or maybe he was just sick of lying.

'You know?'

'Yes, I do.'

'You figured it out?'

'Not completely.'

'What don't you know?'

'Exactly who did it and how.'

He smiled. 'That's everything, Tamara.' He took a sip of coffee, but his hand was shaking.

'Don't bullshit me, Ben.' I had never been more serious about anything in my life. He stopped smiling.

'We all did it,' he said. 'Gus pulled the trigger, but we all did it.' The words hung there for a while in the silence of the room, and I felt tears coming into my eyes, so I didn't look at him. 'That makes us all accessories, doesn't it? Vera wouldn't have anything to do with it or me when she found out about it.'

'And that was why she left you.'

'That was why she left me.' He eased back in his chair, his eyes cast down. 'It's no use hiding it any more, is it?'

'Not unless you plan to kill me too.'

'Tamara—'

I ignored the hurt look on his face and continued. 'Did Gus kill Gina too?'

'His own daughter? How could you say something like that? No, of course not. Gus didn't kill Gina. How could he? But he killed Shawn Raymond because she couldn't leave him alone, that was the truth of it. Gus didn't see it that way. But that was the truth. Gina couldn't leave Shawn alone, even after that last thing that happened.'

My eyes must have told him I knew what that last thing was, how Shawn had used his 'bitch' to entertain his friends, and he shook his head in a way that said he was still astonished

190

and disgusted by what had happened. 'It wouldn't have stopped there,' he said, not looking at me, his voice breaking as he explained it. 'He would have put her on the block before it was over. That was the next step. Right on the block like his mama used to be, selling her body to please him, because she couldn't, wouldn't leave him alone. That was it. That and the drugs. A nasty bastard like that.' He paused, looking around the room as if he had lost something. 'Is it too early for some of that brandy we had last night?' Without answering him, I went into the living room where I'd left the bottle, remembering last night for a moment, and shut out that memory as I sat back down across from him and poured a shot into his cup.

'Gus knew he had to kill him. Because he knew that if he didn't Shawn would destroy Gina and maybe even take Lena along for the hell of it. Gus has been around long enough to know what they look for in a murder investigation: who has the motive, means, and opportunity – isn't that what the cops say? Everybody knew he had the first two – motive and means – in spades, so he had to get rid of the opportunity, not only his but everybody else's. You can't shoot somebody in Newark if you're on a cruise ship in the Caribbean.

'He and Mattie had taken the same Panama Canal cruise about two years ago, so they knew the routine. So when Lena told him what Shawn had done to Gina, and then he found out she was pregnant, and that she would be tied to the son of a bitch for the rest of her life, he knew what he had to do.'

'So he told you what he was planning?'

'Yeah.'

'And what did you do?'

'Everything I could to help him.'

'And killing Shawn Raymond was the only alternative?'

'I was with Gus the night we went to see the son of a bitch.

He just laughed in our faces, spat in our faces, and told us he could put her on the street if he wanted to, he had that much control, and I saw the way Gus looked at the dude. I knew then that he was going to do something. I just didn't know what.' Ben paused long enough to take a swallow of his spiked coffee, and added another shot.

'So he made the reservations for all of us, including me and Vera. And then he got himself a fake passport. A retired cop knows enough people in and outside the law who know how to do it, and it's easy enough to do. They sell them, for one thing, if you know where to look. But Gus went down South, to rural Mississippi, found himself one of those hundred-year-old black churches with an old graveyard attached, like the ones those rednecks were burning a while back, and found the grave of a child who was born the same year as him but died soon after. The powers that be in those places don't give a damn about black folks, living or dying, so they didn't bother keeping up-to-date records of births or deaths or anything like that. The only records kept were church records, or on tombstones or in family Bibles. So he got a birth date and then he got a birth certificate based on church records and a faked affidavit that nobody would check. If you have a birth certificate, you can get a passport no questions asked.'

'He covered his bases.'

Ben smiled ironically. 'If you plan to kill somebody and not get caught, you better cover your bases.'

'So he got on the *Odyssey* with two passports. One real and the other fake,' I said, filling that in for him.

'We had a reservation for a table for four – me, Mattie, Gus, and Vera. Gus made a big thing out of talking and joking with the waiters and maître d' every night so they'd remember him. About the third night into the cruise, he didn't show up one night for dinner, and Mattie said he had stomach problems and got food sent to his room.'

'And then came the morning of April twenty-fifth.'

'Yeah,' Ben said, avoiding my eyes, not wanting to talk about it, or maybe even think about it. 'He'd called a friend of his on the force and made up some bullshit about Zeke so he would be picked up and put in jail on suspicion for a couple of days, and that took care of his brother's alibi. He chose the twenty-fifth because it was Claudia Holly's birthday, and Mattie strongly encouraged Lena and Gina to go over with this basket of food to surprise Claudia. She even paid for it all, and told Claudia's mother they were planning this surprise so they'd feel obligated to do it. That gave them both an alibi. Lena could have guessed that something was up, but nothing was actually said to her.'

I remembered what Claudia had said about how concerned Lena was when Gina decided to get ice at the last minute. She wanted to make sure that her sister would be inside and accounted for if something actually happened.

'Gina didn't suspect anything when Shawn died?'

'Gina wasn't stupid, just foolish. I'm sure it occurred to her, but what could she do?'

Die for it, you lying bastard, I thought about saying but didn't. I just kept calm, and as distant as I could. 'How exactly did Gus do it?'

Ben closed his eyes again, those pretty lashes reminding me of our ride over in the car and how touched I had been by his vulnerability. I felt a stab of sadness and regret at what might have been between us but was gone now forever. He felt it too. I could hear that in his voice and see it in his eyes. He sighed a heavy sigh, then told it straight with no emotion or hesitation.

'We docked at eight in the morning in Cartagena, and we all

left the boat for sightseeing at around nine, after breakfast. Gus made a point that morning of refusing any food and casually complaining to the waiter that his stomach was acting up again. He got off the ship with everybody else, and then later when new crew members came on duty, the three of us, Mattie and then me and Vera, drifted back on board. Gus was on his way out of Cartagena on a chartered plane with his fake passport to San Juan by then, and by three he was leaving San Juan to fly back to New York.'

'Nobody stopped him, questioned his fake passport?'

'He left from Cartagena, Tamara, *Cartagena!* If they had, he had enough American dollars to bribe anybody who needed to be bought. He carried a lot of cash, and he was dressed like a tourist. Nobody looks that much at a tourist's passport.

'Gus had rented a car in New York City using his fake name and passport, using cash for everything he did, and the car was waiting for him in the long-term parking lot. He'd put the gun, an unlicensed .38 that couldn't be traced, in .the glove compartment. By the time the rest of us sat down to dinner at eight on the *Odyssey*, lying to the waiter about Gus's indigestion, he was on his way to Newark to kill Shawn Raymond.'

'With a shot right through the heart, like an expert marksman.' I remembered my thoughts when Osborne told me about the shot that had killed him. I also realised that if Shawn Raymond had had any last-minute doubts, any sudden intuitive warnings that his hours were numbered, Gus's voice on the other side of the door was almost identical to his brother Chee-chee's, so he would have suspected nothing.

'He flew back to San Juan early that next morning, and then from there to the San Blas Islands in Panama, where the ship docked that morning. We all got back on the boat at different times but were all there for dinner, in time to smile and joke with the waiters. He ordered a bottle of expensive champagne to toast the Panama Canal when we sailed through it the next day.' He paused then, emptying his coffee cup. 'I guess Gus was right, huh?'

'About what?'

'He knew I'd tell you sooner or later. Couldn't you tell how scared he was of our relationship developing, of what it might become?'

'He was the one who suggested you call me, wasn't he?'

'He had no idea it would go this far, that once I started with you I wouldn't be able to stop.'

'And you're saying now that this whole thing between us was real for you?'

'Yes. Wasn't it for you?'

'You lied to me, Ben, about something so basic, so . . .' I grasped for words, but couldn't find any. 'What was all that shit about truthfulness and sick of playing games, and—' I stopped myself then, letting it all go, controlling my anger, my disappointment, and the dreams I'd allowed myself to have for these few weeks. Two people were dead. They had both been murdered. It was obscene to think about some silly, romantic fantasy I'd concocted about what could have been.

'Tamara, please—' Ben said. I held up my hands to stop him from continuing, but he finished anyway. 'I know I have no right to expect anything from you now. But the truth of it is, Tamara, that whatever happens, I'm glad we had what we did. I'm glad I told you. I'm glad it's finally off my chest.'

'Off your chest!' I said in astonishment. 'Ben, it's more than just off your chest now.' *Can he possibly think that this confession is all there is to it?* I wondered. *That I'll keep my mouth shut about it? That he, Gus, Mattie, and even his wife will walk away from Shawn Raymond's murder scot-free?*

195

'I understand that.' The scared, desperate look in his eyes and the tremble in his voice told me he understood only too well.

'And you were going to let somebody else pay for it.' He looked at me like he didn't quite understand, then replied with an edge to his voice that made me wary.

'Can we just let it drop?'

'Drop?' I glared at him in amazement and continued. 'You and Gus were willing to let some kid, some poor nameless kid, spend the rest of his young life in jail for something the two of you did?'

'But isn't that the operative word, Tamara, "nameless"?' He must have seen the disgust in my eyes because he dropped his as if he was ashamed now for that part of it too. 'There just didn't seem to be any other way out.'

'There's always a way out.'

'No. Sometimes there isn't.'

I stood up slowly. He stood with me.

A killer is a killer. Even if he didn't hold the gun. Even if you've just spent the night with him. My breath got tight as I studied Ben Lennox. I tried to push the panic down as I wondered if I was in more danger than I thought. He was a big man, a solidly built man, and those strong manicured hands that had caressed me so gently last night were suddenly menacing and frightening.

And who would know?

I'd been so cute and cagey with Annie about last night, she didn't know a damn thing, not even his name. But Jamal knew. My stomach knotted and I felt my throat constrict. So if Gus or Ben killed me they would have to take my son out too. I thought about that gun I keep locked up in my closet in the box with the combination lock, the thing I never think about unless

196

I have to. Ben glanced at me with a sardonic smile on his lips as if he knew what was on my mind.

'I'm not going to hurt you, Tamara. Don't you know what kind of man I am?'

'I know exactly what kind of man you are.'

'You should know that much. At least what kind of man I am, after all these weeks, after last night,' he continued like he didn't hear me.

'I don't know anything any more.'

I backed away from him. He moved toward me as if he might try to touch me, but then he sat back down, placing his hands in front of him flat on the table, like a man does when he surrenders, letting me know that he would not use them against me. I stood where I was, my eyes not leaving his.

'I couldn't hurt you, Tamara. And I don't regret anything else. I don't regret helping Gus. He was just protecting his family, that was all. A man has a right to protect what is his.'

'What is *his*, Ben? What exactly is that right? To completely control another person? To take somebody's life because they aren't what they should be? Gina was not a child. She was a woman who made stupid, fatal choices, but they were her choices to make. Gus Lennox had no right to kill a man, even a man like Shawn Raymond, because of them.'

'Shawn Raymond deserved to die.' He set his face into a stubborn mask.

'Who the hell was Gus, or you, to decide that?'

'But don't you see, don't you understand?' his eyes and voice pleaded. 'Everything would have been all right if it hadn't come back at us like it did with Gina.'

'Did you actually think you could kill somebody and *not* have it come back at you?'

* * *

197

We sat there for a while before I handed him the telephone. He looked at me, knowing what I expected of him, his eyes begging me not to make him take that step, hoping I would change my mind.

'You do it, Ben, or I will,' I told him, and listened as he called the local precinct and told the officer who picked up the phone that he had crucial information on a murder that he wanted to give to them. Then he called a lawyer he knew in South Orange and told him what he had done and that he needed some legal counsel, and asked if he could pick him up at my place and take him to the precinct. And then he called Gus. 'I told her,' was all he said.

We didn't speak to each other as we waited for his attorney to pick him up, Ben sipping the brandy straight now, me wishing this day had never happened.

'Tamara.' He said my name tenderly, as seductively as he'd whispered it last night.

'Yes, Ben.'

'I'm sorry.'

'So am I.'

'Do you have any idea who killed my niece?' He posed the question more to himself than to me. I didn't reply, even though I knew the answer.

Follow the money is what they tell you to do if you want to find a murderer. 'Follow the grief,' were the words that came to my mind, and that would lead me straight back to where I started.

Twelve

It was the gun that told me. It had been a .38 fired straight and sure by somebody aiming for her heart, the way he had aimed at mine that night. A kid turning fast and shooting in front of him. Bessie had told me that the truth was all she had, and that she was willing to face it, but as I drove to her cramped apartment in that once elegant building, I knew that this particular truth would be more bitter than any she could have imagined.

Viola Rudell had been right without even knowing why.

Shawn Raymond is dead because of that rich bitch Gina Lennox. I say that out loud to myself and to my boy a hundred times a day.

How many times had she thrown Gina's baby into Rayshawn's face, cursed Gina's name? And her family, "them hincty niggers over there off Bergen"? She had planted the seeds. They had grown, bloomed, and borne fruit when her son murdered Gus Lennox's daughter the night before last on the sidewalk in front of his home. Rayshawn Rudell had been headed for that moment from the first night I saw him. He had probably hidden that gun like young boys hide dirty magazines – sneaking a look at them now and again before they go to bed at night. He had practised with it – savouring the power it gave him, the kind of power he'd felt when he pulled it out at me,

199

making him feel more like his outlaw father. He knew how Gina looked because he knew how Lena looked. Had he followed her one day, spotting her by chance, or parked himself on Bergen till he caught a glimpse of her, then stalked her, figuring out how he could get to her? It had taken him time, but he had gotten a kid's stupid, jealous revenge.

Tears came to my eyes as I recalled the pride with which Bessie Raymond had pulled out his photo that day in my office, her fearful, haunted look when she sensed I had something terrible to tell her about him, and the bounce in her voice when she reported that she and Viola had agreed to send him away in the spring. It was too late for that now.

My silence about Rayshawn Rudell's gun had caused Gina's death.

Guilt ripped through me, leaving me feeling sick and disgusted with myself. I slammed on my brakes in front of Bessie's building, hitting the curve and driving my front wheels on to the sidewalk, my own anguish rising in my throat like bile. The dull grey vestibule of her building was silent and empty as I bolted to her apartment, and I slowed my pace, wondering what in God's name I would tell this woman, trying to search for the words that would hurt her the least. But there were no words I could say. My heart beat fast as I rang her doorbell, listening for her footsteps.

'Who is there?' Her voice was low and frightened, suspicious.

'Tamara Hayle.'

'What do you want?'

'Bessie, I have something important to talk to you about.'

'Ain't you told me everything important you had to tell me?' I detected a hostility in her voice that made me uneasy.

'Bessie, please let me in. I've learned something that – that

I think you should know. That it's my responsibility to tell you.'
I spoke firmly, reminding myself of my duty to her as well.

'Like who killed my son?'

'Yes. But there is more too.'

I heard her snap the bolt open, and then she slipped the chain
on and opened the door just enough to see my face.

'Tell me now.'

'You don't want to hear this from me standing out here in
the hall. Let me come inside.'

She opened the door and I stepped inside as she quickly
closed it behind me. The long, narrow hall where we stood
seemed darker than it had that first time, or maybe we were
just lingering there longer. She had been eager to share what
she could that day, and had hurried me into the living room.
She had had tears in her eyes then, and she had been crying
again today. But there was something different about her, about
the way she wouldn't quite look at me and the stiff, strained
way she held her body. Something was wrong. I stopped short,
my body tuned for danger as my sixth sense whispered a
warning.

'You wanted to get in here, now you're in here,' Bessie
Raymond said with a strange finality. Her eyes were wide and
her voice was unnaturally loud, as if she were trying to prove
something to someone. 'What else do you know?'

I put my fear aside. She was dressed as she had been the
day I met her, that lime-green maid's uniform rustling loosely
around her skinny body.

'I know who really killed your son.'

'What else?'

There was no anticipation, excitement, or even relief when I
said it, no quick demand to know. But her chin was trembling,
and her voice was filled with trepidation. I spoke straight

because there was no gentle way to put it.

'Gus Lennox killed Shawn. He was on a cruise and he flew back to New York, then drove to Newark and shot him.' Bessie drew in a fast breath, and let it out a little at a time, a sob hanging to the end of it. She rocked back as if I had punched her.

'What else?' She quickly composed herself, throwing that question out there again. I could see within her eyes, set so deep in her dark brown face, the eyes of her son and her grandson. Those eyes hardened, and I could get no sense of what was on her mind. But then she gave a quick, furtive glance behind her. I knew what she was trying to hide.

Rayshawn was here, and Viola was probably with him, because she knew that Bessie loved her son as much as she did, and would protect him with her last breath if need be and by any means that she could. My body grew tense as I listened for the sound in the kitchen or bedroom that would tell me where they were.

'What else?' Bessie demanded to know.

It was then that Viola stepped into my view. I wasn't surprised to see her or the gun – the .38-calibre snub-nosed Colt – that she held in her small hands. She used it to motion me into the living room, and I did what she said as I tried to pretend that I didn't see that gun.

'What else?' Viola asked Bessie's question.

'You know what else,' I said.

'What else? Tell me.'

'How often did you tell him that Gina Lennox was responsible for his father's death? How often did you throw that woman's name up in his face?' Nothing about Viola changed, not her voice, face, or stance. It was as if she hadn't heard me.

I edged toward her, taking a chance. I was bigger than her by almost a foot, and stronger. But she was a fighter, she had told me that, and I hadn't gone mano a mano with anybody – big, tough man or scrappy little woman – in a long time.

'I'm not going to let them take Rayshawn. If I have to kill you or anybody else standing in this room to keep them from doing that, I will.' She spoke with the calm assurance of someone who knows that nothing outside of death will defeat her. I knew how far she would go to protect her son, because I knew how far I would go to protect mine. There had been a paranoid, persecuted tone in her voice in that first talk we'd had in her apartment, and I heard it again now, and saw it in her eyes as they darted around the room.

'Let me talk to Rayshawn, maybe we can—'

'You won't take him!'

I could hear Bessie breathing behind me. I could see her out of the corner of my eyes. Was she willing to kill me to protect her grandson? Was she on my side or on Viola's?

'Bessie?' I said her name, whispering it as if she were the only one who could hear me, and turned slightly, catching her eye. I could see fear in them too. Was she afraid of Viola? Maybe she always had been.

'You brought him here to protect him, didn't you?' I said to Viola, trying hard not to look at the gun. 'But Rayshawn is a minor, if—'

'*No!*' Viola screamed the word out, cutting me off. 'I'll kill him before I let them have him.' Bessie drew in a breath.

'Don't say that, Viola,' I said.

'I'll take him myself before I let you or anybody else take him.' And she would do it, I was sure of that. For spite and in desperation. She was capable of killing me, Bessie, her son, and then herself if she saw no other way out.

Why don't you ask the bitch who wears it?

'Ma,' Rayshawn said, and the room turned still as each of us, women with sons, responded to that word and the voice teetering on the edge of manhood that spoke it. Viola flinched visibly, and my fear and love for my own son stirred through my bones. 'Ma, why you want to say something like that? Why you want to say something like that about me?' His plea verged on a cry.

'Get back in the bedroom, Rayshawn.' The desperation in her voice frightened me more than anything else. 'Get back in that room!'

'He didn't mean to do it, Viola,' I said. 'They'll all understand. Nobody will take him away from you. Nobody can.'

'Get back in the room, Rayshawn!' she ordered him.

'Put the gun down, Viola,' Bessie said from behind me, moving in front of me, toward Viola. 'You never did my son no good, don't think you will hurt my grandson. Put it down.'

Now Rayshawn moved toward his mother too, glancing at her and then at me for some kind of answer, his eyes hopeless and empty.

'Don't say nothing, Rayshawn,' Viola said.

'Tell us, baby. Please tell us,' Bessie begged him, and I knew then she was on my side. Rayshawn's eyes grew wide with confusion and apprehension.

'Mama said where she lived and I just wanted to see it, to see where the baby lived. She told me I wasn't nothing to him. She said he didn't even know who I was.'

'And you were mad because you loved and miss your father?' *Son.*

I could see his answer in his eyes.

'You had the gun because you always carry the gun.' I said it for him. He looked even younger and more desperate than he had the first time I'd set eyes on him, but his face this time was filled with bewilderment, not the menacing arrogance that had greeted me then. He stood slightly behind his mother now. I caught his eyes and held them as I spoke.

'You didn't mean to kill her, did you? He's a minor,' I said to Viola. 'Maybe there are things that can be done—' I stopped because I had no idea what they were. He had taken a woman's life. Maybe Jake would know what to do and say about the law. I had no idea. Rayshawn sensed my misgivings. He moved closer to Viola, seeking her protection.

'I didn't mean to kill her,' he muttered, his eyes cast to the floor.

'Put it down,' Bessie said to Viola, drawing my attention to her once again. 'Just put it down, Viola. Put it down.' There was a threat of violence in her voice, and her eyes were fastened on Viola's face.

'If I have to kill you too, old bitch, I'll kill you too. I won't let them take him.'

Bessie moved toward her then. There was no fear in her eyes, and her voice was as clear and calm as I'd ever heard it.

'You think everything was stole from you, Viola Rudell? Everything was stole from *me*. From his daddy's blood running red down that nasty Prince Street to now, to this minute. Shawn was all I got from Antoine. Rayshawn is all I got from Shawn. Goddamn you, Viola, give me the gun!'

Viola stepped back as Bessie advanced toward her, the gun still held straight in front of her. I thought for a moment she would shoot her. Her grip had tightened: her body seemed tense, looking for some violent release. But then she lowered the gun, and Bessie reached down and took it as easily as if she were shaking hands.

And it was over.

'I done seen enough evil in my life from this thing. I don't even want to hold it,' Bessie muttered, her eyes closed as she passed the weapon to me.

We all stood motionless then, afraid to move or speak, none of us quite believing that the powerful emotions we had felt just moments before – the terror and rage, the violent urge to protect – could so easily and quickly disappear. The hand that held the gun now rested at Viola's side, her fingers still in a claw. Bessie, with an anguished look on her face, had found a cigarette somewhere and was sucking the smoke into her body in tight, fast draws. I took the bullets out of the gun, my eyes focused on what I was doing, not wanting to look at or even think about what had just happened between us. Viola was the first to move. She slumped down on the couch, and began to cry. Bessie slid down beside her, comforting her, her arm over Viola's shoulder, taking her sobs into her body as if they were her own. I stood for a while, still holding the gun, and then finally sat down myself, trying to catch my breath, to find some calm within me. And there we stayed for the next ten minutes, three women, three mothers – one whose son had been murdered, one whose son was a murderer, and me, more aware than I'd ever been of the traps that wait to claim the lives of young black men, and wondering if I could always protect my own.

Rayshawn, the centre of all that had happened, had collapsed where he stood and was holding his head in his hands. Maybe for the first time he fully understood what had happened, what he had done. I wondered what would become of him, if he would end up like his father, like his grandfather, if it was too late to do anything about it.

I called Jake then, and within half an hour he had come to Bessie's apartment and the five of us – Jake, Viola, and

Rayshawn in Jake's car and me and Bessie in mine –
accompanied him to the police station so that Rayshawn could
turn himself in. Viola stayed for a while at Jake's office to talk
with him about Rayshawn. I drove Bessie home. When she
asked me to come upstairs because she didn't want to be by
herself, I went in with her.

I had to fit that last piece of the puzzle Bessie had tossed me
where it belonged. When she went into her bedroom to change
her clothes, I picked up the photograph that was perched in its
silver frame on the television and studied it as if I'd never seen
it before. The face and body of Antoine Raymond had been
blurred with age and handling. There was no way to make out
that elaborate 'P' cut as deeply into his arm as a burn unless I
knew what to look for. It was the same mark, that 'P' I'd seen
on Zeke's arm and assumed was a scar, the same one that was
probably carved somewhere on Gus.

'P' for the Prince Street Gang.

'Shawn's father?'

'I told you it was.'

'How did he die?'

'I told you that too, don't you remember?' Bessie pushed
out the smoke from her cigarette as hard as if she were pushing
out every bit of trouble she'd ever met. 'I told you that the first
day I talked to you. Died by the gun, and now damned if his
son didn't go out the same goddamn way.'

'Who shot him?' I watched her face carefully, wondering if
she knew what I did, if I should tell her if she didn't.

She shrugged. 'One of them no-good thugs he hung with. I
never could find out which one. Damn cops wouldn't tell me
shit. Never did, never would. They sent some of them to jail,
though. Antoine was the only one who paid for all their
stupidness, all their meanness with his sweet life. That seem to

207

be the luck of the Raymonds, don't it?' She gave a rueful cackle.

'Remember I asked you about Chee-chee?' Carefully I placed the photograph back where I'd gotten it, choosing my words carefully too.

'Chee-chee?' The same puzzled expression that had come to her face the first time I mentioned it came again. 'Never heard of him.'

'I found out that Chee-chee was a friend of Shawn's. But his real name was Zeke. Zeke Lennox. Did Shawn ever mention him to you?'

'No.'

'He was Gina Lennox's uncle. Did Antoine ever mention somebody named Zeke to you?'

'Gina Lennox had an uncle named Chee-chee?' she asked, still not fully comprehending.

'Shawn never mentioned anybody named Zeke or Chee-chee either?'

'Shawn never told me his business.'

'Did Antoine ever mention somebody named Zeke?' I asked again.

She sighed and shook her head. 'That was a long time ago, baby. A long time ago.'

'Try to remember, Bessie.'

She thought for a moment, her hand fluttering to her mouth and back again, and then she smiled. 'Seems like he did hang out with somebody with a strange name like that. Pushed-in face, kind of like one of them little dogs rich ladies carry? Zeke? It seemed like Antoine did used to fool around with somebody whose name began with a Z, I know that. They used to always be kidding each other about how they were trouble from A to Z. It could have been Zeke, ain't too many other names I can think of start with Z. Did he have something to do with killing

Shawn. Did he?' Her eyes narrowed and her body stiffened, ready to attack or curse somebody out.

'No,' I said. 'I think he considered Shawn his friend.'

And maybe in his own way, he had – after his brother had shot Shawn's father, after prison and the troubles the 'bad' brother had seen. Who knew where they had crossed paths, Zeke Lennox and Shawn Raymond? Maybe in jail serving time together, or walking down some short mean street on a Saturday night. Shawn looked like Antoine Raymond, had his style from what I could tell in that picture. But maybe it had been his eyes that told Zeke his mother was Bessie Raymond. Antoine's brown-skinned, light-eyed wife. Shawn's face may have brought Zeke's past back to him as quickly and with as much power as Rayshawn's had brought mine back to me.

Had Zeke tried to befriend Shawn Raymond, making amends in his own clumsy way for the life his brother had taken? Or had their relationship been one of simple convenience, that of a user of drugs to a dealer? When had Zeke shared the facts of their old connection? During some drunken jag or drug-induced confession? However things had happened between them, Shawn had avenged his father's death by abusing Gus's favorite daughter, and he had paid for it with his life, and then been avenged himself by his son, who would pay in one way or another for the rest of his.

'So they went back, Zeke and Shawn and Antoine,' Bessie said slowly, as if she was beginning to understand some new truth, and then she shook her head as if getting rid of thoughts that she wasn't going to share. 'When I think of Rayshawn killing that sweet girl, taking my grandbaby's mother from him, I feel so ashamed I don't think I can live with it. You think them Lennoxes can forgive me for what Rayshawn done to their daughter?'

'If you can forgive them for what Gus Lennox did to your son.'

'It don't never seem to end, do it?' Bessie said, and she took my hand in hers and held it until she felt strong enough to let it go.

Epilogue

'I'm as guilty as everybody else. I knew about that damn gun. I could have saved Gina Lennox's life. I can't forgive myself for that.' Jake and I sat across from each other as Ben and I had earlier, except it was late, and we'd been here for the better part of two hours and I had been beating myself up for most of it. Every part of me – body and soul – was aching. 'Sooner or later a kid with a gun is going to use it. If I had just told the police like I was supposed to do. If I had just—'

'There are always ifs, Tamara. If Zeke hadn't joined the Prince Street Gang, then Gus wouldn't have had to betray him. If Gus hadn't killed Antoine Raymond, then his son might not have turned bad. If Shawn hadn't hooked up with Zeke, then Gina Lennox might still be alive. You can't think about the ifs because there is no way to change things. What's done is done.'

'But if only I had gone to the cops—'

'How many times have you told me you don't trust cops? You did what you thought was right at the time and that's all you can expect of yourself. Let it go.' He smiled that wise, pensive smile that always charms me. But all I felt was sorrow.

'I can't stop thinking about Gina.'

'Gina was everybody's victim. Her father, her lover, his son. I think about Gina and all I want to do is go home and put my arms around Denice.'

'What will happen to Rayshawn?'

Jake turned serious. 'He took Gina's life, but he's only thirteen, and a child has to be at least fourteen to be tried as an adult in this state, which plays in his favor. He could end up doing twenty years in a juvenile facility, or, if he can prove that he has changed for the better and his life is "redeemable", he could get out when he turns eighteen. It pretty much depends on who he has in his corner.'

'Viola will have to get herself together enough to be there for him.'

'I've seen this kind of thing turn around a family before. I've also decided to take the case pro bono,' he added.

'Thanks, Jake.' His shrug told me that there was nothing to thank him for. 'And Mattie and Lena and Ben? What will happen to them?' I avoided his eyes when I mentioned Ben, not ready to think or talk about him yet.

'Gus will take on as much of the guilt and blame as he can. Whatever lies he has to tell to protect his family, he will tell them. I do know that much about the man.'

I didn't ask about Bessie Raymond because I knew the answer. Our lives were tied by Johnny in the past and Rayshawn in the present, and I couldn't, in good faith, break that bond again. I would be there for her and hers whenever she needed me. Johnny's debt would finally be repaid.

'Well, maybe there is one good thing that has come from all this.'

'What's that?' Jake asked.

'Bessie Raymond will finally get to see her grandbaby.' We both smiled at that. They had all been torn by so much hatred, violence, and grief, it was time for a little love to poke its way into their lives.